Contents

Jungle Series

Written By LI DI

Haqi the Leopard

A story about
misunderstanding and love

Prunus Press USA

Original Title:《豹子哈奇》

Original book by The Writers Publishing House Co.,Ltd.

This edition is published by arrangement with Prunus Press USA, through the agency of China National Publications Import and Export (Group) Co., Ltd.

All rights reserved.

HAQI THE LEOPARD

Written by Li Di

Translated by Haiwang Yuan

Designed by Brandy Ding

First edition 2022

ISBN: 978-1-61612-143-3

Prunus Press USA

Whoever is kind-hearted
Is the best person in the world.

—from an Aini folksong

Part I

The Leopard
Family

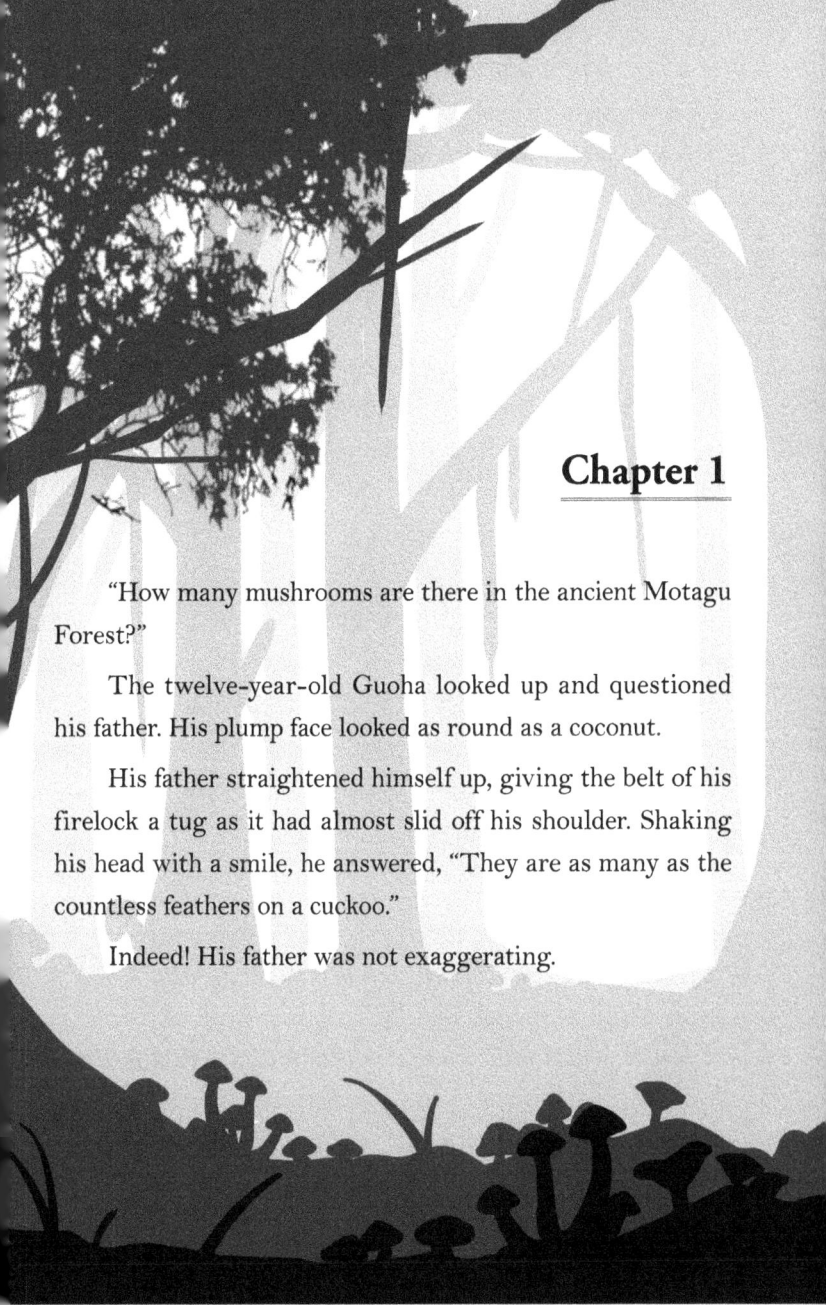

Chapter 1

"How many mushrooms are there in the ancient Motagu Forest?"

The twelve-year-old Guoha looked up and questioned his father. His plump face looked as round as a coconut.

His father straightened himself up, giving the belt of his firelock a tug as it had almost slid off his shoulder. Shaking his head with a smile, he answered, "They are as many as the countless feathers on a cuckoo."

Indeed! His father was not exaggerating.

Look at the quilted green russula mushrooms under the amazingly fast-growing bur-flower tree. Like boys and girls wearing light green hats, they danced around it hand in hand. Look at the gray Bolete mushrooms under the kapok tree. Like humpbacked old men dressed in black, they appeared to be enjoying the sight of the red flowers all over the tree. Look at the winter mushrooms seemingly playing hide-and-seek with Guoha behind the buttress roots of the big banyan tree. Not only did they have a wonderful taste and smell, but they would also leave a lingering scent on the hands after touching them. Look at the plain and yet charmingly naïve tuber mushrooms. They stood quietly in the grass holding their large brown umbrellas. Look at the "chicken-feet" mushrooms cockily sticking out their necks to look around. They made sure that little Guoha would notice them and know that they could be as delicious as the meat of chickens. Look! There were also the mushrooms called the lurid bolete, the saffron milk cap, and those with the locals' nicknames "muntjac's head" and "pine's hair"…

Mushrooms were so many here, scattering in clusters all over the pine forest like stars crowding the sky.

Guoha and his father each collected a pack basket of mushrooms in the forest before long.

Guoha felt so happy that he could not help leaping and hopping as he tagged after his father. The two rows of round, silver buttons on his short, black shirt were jingling against each other.

"Dad! Mom must be very happy when she is back from herding our goats and sees us with so many mushrooms."

Before Father had time to reply, Guoha suddenly turned his head toward the depth of the forest. Listening for a while, he said, his eyes widening, "Dad, listen! Someone is crying there, 'Come …! Come …!'"

Father broke into a smile, his eyes squinting below his thick and dark brows that flapped down like the wings of a hawk. He chuckled, "Hehe! Your ears are as sharp as those of a young leopard cat. It's not a person who's crying. It's the Motagu Forest."

"Motagu Forest is crying?"

"Yes. A big wind is rising from the Nanla Mountain, and it is blowing through the forest and rustling the leaves. Listening from a distance, it sounds like the crying of a person."

Before Father finished, a flock of scarlet finches fluttered by shrieking in panic. They flew barely above the heads of Guoha and his father and nearly brushed the tips of the tree branches. Meanwhile, out of the huge mesh of elephant creepers and Chinese chestnut trees there jumped two long-necked, thin-legged red deer one after the other. Seeing Guoha and his father in their way, they froze for a second, blinking their eyes as dark as black grapes, and turned to a narrow path tramped by animals. They quickly leapt into the thick brushes, leaving a series of crackling sounds behind.

A few muffled growls came from the old forest a few yards away, causing the ground to shiver.

Grabbing his father's brawny, veiny hand and held it tight, Guoha asked, "Dad! Dad! What's that sound?"

"It sounds like some beasts are fighting each other,"

replied father; the wrinkles on his broad, tanned chest suddenly appeared more distinctive.

"Let's go and take a look."

As he said so, father held his firelock tight against his back with one hand and took Guohua's with the other. "Let's drive them away with the report of our firelock. What's point of fighting when you have a good life to enjoy?"

Leading Guoha with his hand, Father waded through the thick bushes and entangled vines. They arrived at the source of the fighting growls.

A terrible battle had just ended.

In the twilight of the dusk, a 300-pound wild boar was lying on the grassy ground covered with trampled branches from the bushes.

It was a male wild boar.

It was covered with blood, its back and belly torn open and looking messy. Blood was gushing from the cut on its neck, and it opened like a big mouth. A large tract of the grassy ground had turned red.

The wild boar was apparently dead with its sword-like tusks pointing up as if in defiance.

About a dozen steps away lay a female leopard. Its beauti-fully-spotted fur was smeared with black and purple patches, its entrails sprawling beneath its belly.

Apparently, its belly had been torn open by the tusks of the wild boar.

The leopard had barely breathed its last breath, its hind

legs still twitching slightly.

A fierce battle had cost both the animals dearly.

What implacable hatred would have led the two great beasts of the Motagu Forest to their fatal encounter?

"We came too late," murmured Father in sorrow.

Guoha was still dumbfounded.

It was the first time for him to witness a bloody fight between two animals.

His young heart was thumping and thumping.

A cool breeze swept through the ancient forest. It shook the leaves, and their whisper sounded like a lament for the death of the two animals.

"Dad, why did they fight?" asked Guoha while shaking his father's hand.

"Well, you are right. Why?"

Father breathed a big sigh.

He turned his sight away from the leopard and redirected it to the rolling Nanla Mountain through the thick foliage of the ancient forest.

The once lush Nanla Mountain now looked like a person's head infested with boils that had left bald patches after healing. They were marks of blind human efforts to cut down the trees in order to farm. They had felled tracts of the forests. They had set fire to them and let them burn for a few days and nights. Then, in the fields covered with ashes, they began to grow some economic crops with names hard to pronounce.

Countless animals eking out their existence from the

forests had perished in the smoke and fire without reason.

Slashing and burning, how stupid these people were! Eventually, they had to pay for what they had done to Mother Nature.

Father pulled his sight slowly back from the Nanla Mountain to look at the leopard lying in a pool of blood.

"By destroying the forests to get land for farming, humans are already risking your lives. But why on earth do you have to kill each other?"

Saying so, squatted down by the leopard and caressed its furry body.

"What a shame! It was a beautiful leopard, as beautiful as a shining gem."

Hearing his father's words, Guoha could not help taking a hard look at the leopard.

Suddenly, he shouted in alarm, "Dad! Dad! The leopard's alive. Its eyes are open!"

Holding out his big hand and placed it against the nostrils of the leopard, father shook his head and announced, "It is dead."

"Then, why does it keep its eyes open?"

Guoha insisted on asking his father.

He had so much to learn.

And he wanted to know a lot.

Father said, "When they die, bamboos come into flower. When they pass away, elephants keep their tusks from being found. With its eyes open in death, the leopard must have something to worry about."

The leopard had something to worry about?

What did she worry about?

Stretching its neck forward, the leopard kept its eyes wide open.

What was it looking at?

What was it thinking of?

Soon, the questions were answered…

Searching in the direction of the leopard's gaze with his eyes, Guoha spotted a kitty deep in the grass.

"Look! A kitty! Here's a kitty!"

Upon hearing Guoha's exclamation, father came over. Holding the kitty gently as he rose, father took a close look and smirked.

"This is not a kitty. It's a leopard cub!"

"What? A baby leopard?"

Guoha looked at it with broadened eyes. Wow, sure enough! It was a leopard cub!

The cub was covered with fluffy golden hair, still moist. Its pointed ears were drooping listlessly, its little paws clenched, and its babyish eyes shut.

It was so funny that it had three or four whiskers on both sides of its little pink mouth.

A cute little thing! It was as adorable as pitiful.

"No wonder why the leopard should have fought the boar. As a saying goes, 'Trees sway where there's a wind.'" Father started reasoning, "A tiger would have walked away when it saw a wild boar of this size. The leopard turned out to be the mother of this cub. It might be nursing it when the wild boar showed up in surprise. The leopard mother had thought that the boar was trying to harm its baby. So, it had charged at the boar and got into the brawl. To protect its baby, a leopard mother never considers its own safety. But, it was a tough boar to fight. While beating the boar, the leopard mother also gotten its belly torn open by the boar's tusks. Even with great pain, it had meant to return to its cub, but had collapsed after taking a few steps. It was worrying about its baby, and in death, it still turned its head toward it…"

"Poor leopard mom!" Guoha broke into tears as he acclaimed.

Tears also flooded Father's eyes.

A mountain breeze dried off father's tears.

"Dad, now that it's lost its mother, how can the baby leopard live on?"

"Yes, it will be hard for him to survive. Grass will turn yellow when it's separated from its root."

"Dad, let's save it and take it home."

"Yes," Father nodded and said, "That's exactly what I'm thinking about. It' a life, and we can't see it starve to death. Let's keep it as a kitty."

The leopard cub gave a cry, as if to voice its vote of yes.

Its cry sounded very much like a kitty's mew.

"But," growing a bit worried, Guoha said, "it's not a kitty

after all. What if it bites us?"

"Silly you! How can a baby leopard bite people?"

"What will happen when it grows up?"

"Growing up with us, it may have learned not to bite people. Anyway, since it's a rare animal, we must take good care of it."

Hearing this, Guoha was thrilled.

He stretched his young hands quickly to his father and asked, "Dad, can I hold it?"

Father handed the leopard cub gingerly to Guoha, saying, "Be careful. Don't get it injured."

Rubbing the cub's moist fur gingerly, Guoha asked his father, "How about giving it a name, dad?"

"So, you think it needs a name?"

"Yah! He will then become a member of our family. We all have names, and he ought to have one, too, right?"

"Yes, yes! The trees in the Motagu Forest may be as countless as the hair on an ox's body, and the blades of grass may be as numerous as the dewdrops, but every tree or blade has its name. We ought to give our leopard baby a name."

Father was gazing at the leopard cub with a beaming face for quite a while when he broke the silence himself by saying, "Guoha, since you were the youngest in our family before we added the little leopard to our family, he must have his name with the first part taken from the last part of yours. That's our Hani tradition. So, I would like to call him Haqi."

"Haqi?" Guoha blinked his eyes and continued, "It

means 'we are one family,' right?"

"You're right. In our Hani language, 'qi' stands for 'one family'."

"It's a great name!" Guoha exclaimed with great joy. Placing his lips gently against the leopard cub's ear, he whispered, "Little leopard, we'll call you Haqi from today on. Do you like it. If you do, give us a cry, will you?"

As it happened, the leopard cub uttered a mew…

Then, he lifted his tender paw and gave Guoha a gentle scratch across his nose.

"So, you like the name. That's awesome!"

Guoha heard the leopard cub's reply again. And again, his nose got itchy from the leopard's gentle scratch.

Holding the baby leopard, Guoha repeated his name, "Haqi! Haqi!"

The father and son set out on their journey home, chatting and laughing.

They were not aware of two eyes as bright as lamps in the thick forest. Those eyes were following them every step of their way.

The eyes belonged to the father of the leopard cub—

An old leopard.

Chapter 2

Taking its family—his wife and the newborn cub, Old Leopard had just fled the ancient forests of Nanla Mountain and settled down.

The new mother had still been in her postpartum confinement, a period when new mothers are put on bed rest, and the cub had yet been to open its eyes. They had needed a quiet and cozy home.

But, their home on the Nanla Mountain—a cave surrounded by bushes and a lee against the wind—had been robbed of its tranquility by tree-destroying farmers. From

time to time, billows of smoke had poured into their den.

Humans had been approaching their den with each passing day.

Old Leopard sighed frequently. But, they had to leave no matter how reluctant they felt.

To survive, Old Leopard, taking his wife and baby, left the home in which they had invested so much. They plunged themselves into the endless Motagu Forest, looking for a place. It would be a place away from humans and bad weather, and a place where food and water would be easy to find.

On their way, Old Leopard and its wife held the cub in their mouths by turns. They moved further and further away from their familiar Nanla Mountain. Ahead of them were the thick forests and grassy valleys. They appeared stranger and stranger to them.

The experienced old leopard knew that the forests were full of various kinds of animals. Each kind had its own home range. Each animal leaves a mark one way or another in different parts of the forests. It does so to avoid running into rival animals. It did it also to pass messages to its family members or to exchange information with them.

Wolves usually pee on fallen trees, grotesque stumps, or the stalks of tall grass. Their pee tells of their arrival and their physical conditions.

Rhinoceroses often poo on the side of the path they roam. They want others to know that they are the masters of the passage.

Wild cattle or black bears like to rub their bodies against

trees. By doing so, they leave their odor on them…

Old Leopard was steering its family away from rival animals' home ranges in this strange environment. It was searching for a relatively quiet place to be their new home. Always on high alert, it sniffed its way with its sharp nose, carefully singling out every odor that marked the various places of the forest.

He would stop as soon as it smelled something new and warned its wife of the danger. Then, he chose a different path and resumed the journey. When it picked up odors that were not very fresh, it would become cautious and fumbled its way through the area. When it found odors to be stale, it would take its family across the area at ease. Stale odors meant that their owners had not been to the area for a long time.

When they arrived at a spot where trees were sparse, they went deep into the grass. There, the pangs of hunger hit them hard. The leopard cub was also crying for food.

Smelling no particular odors, Old Leopard decided to stop for a rest.

It asked its wife to breastfeed their baby. Shaking its beautiful long hair on its neck, it felt renewed strength. With it, it was going to look for food in the thick forest.

Before departure, it kissed its wife by rubbing its mouth against its nose, asking it to wait for its quick return in patience.

As it snuck into the thick forest, Old Leopard sensed the smell of a big wild boar.

The odor came from the bottom of a wild loquat. It was fresh and overwhelming.

Here was the home range of the wild boar!

Old Leopard knew that wild boars were ferocious and fought better than tigers and bears.

It was worried about its wife and baby.

But, it was too late.

When it dashed back to the thick grass, its wife had been cut down, and its baby leopard was missing. A perfect family suddenly ceased to exist.

Weeping mournfully, Old Leopard came up to its wife's body and licked the dirt and blood off bit by bit. Tears that it had tried to hold back rolled down its cheeks.

How gorgeous its wife used to be with its beautiful fur!

But now, it had lost its lust, and what's worse, it had been tainted with blood.

Old Leopard remembered vividly the moment when its wife had been out to search for food. It had inadvertently fallen into the trap set by a hunter. Its desperate cry for help had invited both Old Leopard and the hunter, who had been aiming his shotgun at Old Leopard—the first time that it had seen a hunting rifle. But, to rescue its wife, Old Leopard pounced fearlessly on the hunter. Bang! The rifle had fired. Immediately following a puff of an unforgettably pungent smell of gunpowder, Old Leopard had felt a sharp pain on its forehead. Blood had oozed out and down over its eyes.

It had kept itself from falling. It had burst into a more frightful roar, sprung up like a gust of whirlwind, and swooped down toward the hunter. In panic, the hunter had dropped his shotgun into the trap. Without even looking back, the hunter had scampered for life covering the back of his head with his hands. Old Leopard had not bothered to chase him; for, what had been on its mind then was not the hunter. Old Leopard had rubbed off the blood over its eyes with its front paw and started working on rescuing its wife. Though with great pain, it had managed to drag a broken tree into the trap. He had stopped for a rest only three times. Along the broken tree, its wife had climbed up, and with great emotion, they had held each other tight in each other's arms.

But, now! Its wife that it had rescued at the cost of its life was lying motionless forever.

Old Leopard went on licking the blood stains off its wife's body while weeping. After it finished, it dragged its body up a tall leafy tree and place it securely on a crotch covered with thick foliage.

In the past, this had been how Old Leopard had stored its surplus food.

It was doing it now to keep its wife's body from the harm that could be done by vultures, tigers, and pacts of wolves.

The trees were evergreen, and the leaves were verdant.

My dear wife, rest in peace in the evergreen forest. None would disturb you anymore.

Old Leopard said to its wife in silence.

Taking a last look at its wife, it started scampering down the leafy tree.

It was coming down the tree headfirst when it caught sight of a sow wailing over the body of the big male boar.

It had cried for a long time, its voice hoarse, and its eyes dry.

It was the wild boar's wife.

Old Leopard's eyes were filled instantly with the red flame of revenge.

It was absolutely certain that it could overwhelm the sow.

It could attack her from the front and cut its windpipe with a single bite. Or, it could approach it from the rear and broke one of its leg joints.

But, Old Leopard remained still.

It had put out the flame of revenge itself.

Looking up, it fixed its sad eyes on the poor sow.

I can't hurt it. It's innocent. Perhaps, its babies are crying for its milk at home. Those babies have already lost their father. I can't take their mother from them…

Let bygones be bygones.

Revenge leads to more miseries.

Forgiveness allows us to see another day.

The wailing sow was unaware of Old Leopard behind it. Its inconsolable grief blinded it from what was happening in the entire world.

Well, let it alone. Let it weep away all its sorrow.

Old Leopard sighed in a hush and left the big leafy tree tiptoeing.

In the calm and quiet ancient forest, Old Leopard took a deep breath. Immediately, it detected the smell of the leopard cub.

How familiar the odor was! How excited it was to smell it again!

When the leopard cub had been born in the cave den in the Nanla Mountain, its odor had become familiar to its parents.

At the time, the leopard cub's eyes were still closed. Even when they were opened occasionally, they could see nothing. Its hearing was not functioning well enough to hear or catch the signals its parents made.

Its parents could only communicate with it with their sense of smell.

By the same token, the cub could only identify its parents and know their feelings through smell.

Therefore, both the parents and their cub were sensitive to each other's scent.

Only when the cub grew up with wholesome eyesight and hearing could its parents take full advantage of its senses to train it.

Old Leopard traced its cub's scent to Guoha and his father who were hurrying back home. In no time, it located the cub in Guoha's arms.

Old Leopard opened its eyes wide.

It tightened its body.

It raised its front paw.

It was going to take its cub back.

Chapter 3

To get the cub back, Old Leopard had to get close to the two humans walking as they chatted and laughed.

It had to stalk the two human beings.

Old Leopard knew exactly what "stalking" meant.

Stalking had been his most commonly used tactics in hunting.

It believed that the key to the success of this tactic was to go against the wind.

By going against the wind, it could make its stalked prey unaware of its unusual smell.

This was an expensive lesson that it had learned from many of its failed hunting attempts where its prey had escaped after detecting its smell.

At this moment, Old Leopard clearly sensed that it was prowling in the wind.

The wind would pass its odor onto the prey.

It paused frowning.

In fact, it had overestimated humans' keenness of smell.

The development of vision and hearing had dulled humans' sense of smell.

Old Leopard surveyed its surroundings carefully. It decided to get away from the wind flow coming from behind. It planned to outflank Guoha and his father under the cover of the dense trees and bushes. In front them against the wind, it would wait in ambush for the two seemingly fatigued humans to come along.

As soon as it made up its mind, Old Leopard maneuvered to a location in front of Guoha and his father. It was calmly gazing at them walking up.

Then, a cool, moist breeze blew from behind Guoha and his father, bringing the odor of the leopard cub to the nostrils of Old Leopard.

Old Leopard grew tense, fixing its eyes on the cub without a stir.

How am I going to get my baby back in surprise?

Shall I pounce on the two people when they come over and snatch it from them?

But, they are holding it in their arms, and my mouth may miss it if I jump up, pondered Old Leopard. If I should fail the first attempt, I would waste time, and the humans would have a chance for a counterattack.

Then, what would happen next?

No, I must catch my baby leopard with one bite.

To do so, I must swoop down from above.

Looking up, Old Leopard saw a thick, sturdy fork on a cobra's saffron tree right above its head.

Yes! I'll get on to that fork and wait till the two people come over. Then, I will jump out of the blue, snatch the cub, and disappear in the woods.

Mmm, this will be a fail-proof tactic, mused Old Leopard.

Lurking on a tree before launching an attack on an animal the moment it came to under the tree was the tactic that Old Leopard had used in its usual hunting activities. Now, it would use it to rescue its baby.

It was about to climb the tree when it caught a faint and yet pungent smell.

Its hair stood on end instantly.

It is the smell of gunpowder!

Ever since it got shot by a gun trying to save its wife's life, it had remembered the smell of gunpowder belching from a barrel for the rest of its life.

It would never forget the moment when blood oozed from its forehead in the wake of the stinging odor. Until now, it was still hit by dull pain originating from the deep wound whenever it was cloudy or rainy.

This terrible smell put Old Leopard on high alert.

Where can this terrible and hateful smell of gunpowder come in this forest right now?

Old Leopard soon spied the rifle that the adult was carrying on his shoulder as he was walking.

The smell of gunpowder is undoubtedly coming from its barrel.

They have a shotgun!

Old Leopard immediately felt its heart in its mouth.

The cub's mother has died, it thought, and the cub is all we have to pass on our bloodline. I must make sure that nothing bad will happen to it.

If I take it away by attacking the humans, they would definitely fire at me. What if they miss and hit my baby?

If I were hit, how could a frail life like my leopard baby survive?

Old Leopard was at a loss.

It was trembling all over.

It wished that a piece of the sky would fall and squash the two humans to death.

It wished that the ground would collapse to bring the two to their fatal fall.

It hated itself, regretting that he had failed to take its

baby out of danger before the two humans had got hold of it.

Since its encounter with the trap-setting man, it had begun to hate humans. It considered humans detestable.

If humans had not destroyed the forest, its family would not have had to migrate from the Nanla Mountain, its wife would not have died on their way, and their baby would not have been in the hands of these two people.

Now that my poor baby has fallen into human hands, can anything good happen to it?

No. I must fight them at all costs.

If I should fail to get my baby back, and if they should harm it, I would bite them both to death.

Old Leopard had just made a secret decision to fight the two humans regardless of life and death when suddenly...

...its eyes that had been blurred by hatred and anger shone with surprise.

It witnessed an astounding and unbelievable scene unfolding:

In the chilly forest, the two humans who had been walking and talking merrily suddenly halted their steps. The boy who had been holding the leopard cub in his arms handed it to the adult and then unbuttoned his cloth shirt, took it off, bearing his tanned back, and spread it on the ground. The adult stooped low enough to place the cub on the shirt gently. The boy then gingerly wrapped the cub up in his shirt, leaving a small breathing opening at the cub's little nose and mouth. The bare-backed boy then scooped up the buddle and carried it in his arms while saying something to the adult with a smile on his face. The adult also beamed. Then, they went on their journey in the thick, chilly forest…

What! Old Leopard was dumbfounded.

Why would the boy rather bare his back than wrap the cub in his shirt?

In a daze, Old Leopard had a flashback, remembering what had happened…

When gusts of chilly wind had swept into the Nanla Mountain, the cub's mother would had laid at the opening of the cave, holding their baby tight in its bosom…

So people also love the leopard cub as its mother did?

So people also take pity on the young life that has just lost its mother?

While finding it hard to believe, Old Leopard could not come up with a better explanation to what had been happening under its nose.

Completely confused, it did not know what to do.

Watching the boy and the adult drawing close, Old Leopard scrambled into a decision:

I'd better stop taking the risk for now. I'll follow them for a while and see what's going to happen. I'll seek the right moment to take my little leopard away safely.

Thus thinking, Old Leopard hid itself behind a tree and from the sight of the father and son plodding over.

Old Leopard then shadowed them at a distance neither too close nor too far away. It was looking for the best chance to retrieve its baby.

But it did not act, even when it trailed them to their village.

Standing on a hidden mound, it watched the father and son taking the cub to a low-stilted bamboo house in the west of the village.

Behind the bamboo house was a lust forest of hardy banana trees.

Mountain breezes were frolicking in the forest, gently shaking the broad dark green leaves.

Great! Hiding in the slightly swaying hardy-banana forest, I can get closer to the bamboo house.

It was pondering, licking the corner of its mouth with the tip of its tongue when...

...suddenly, it pricked up its ears.

Amid the disorderly and yet apparently complacent prattles of the domestic animals returning from the prairie, there came a feeble cry:

Meow...

It is the leopard cub!

It caused Old Leopard's heart to skip a beat.

Oh no! What's happening to the baby leopard?

Chapter 4

The baby leopard was all right.

As soon as he entered his bamboo house, Guoha warmed the cub in his arms by the fire pit.

Father was busy making a snug bed for the cub with cotton wadding.

However, the leopard cub began to meow after it had been quiet for a while.

Obviously, a warm bed was not quite appealing for now.

"Haqi, stop meowing! You're home. Open your eyes and have a look: This is your home. Here, you won't have to suffer from the wind blowing in the forest."

Haqi kept meowing, as if he had not heard Guoha at all.

The anxious Guoha asked his father, "Dad, why is Haqi crying all the time?"

"Well, he must be hungry," father answered grinning. "When you were hungry as a baby, you cried even worse."

"Aw, aw! It's all right, Haqi. I know you're hungry. Be patient! I'll get you some food right away."

With this, Guoha took from an earthen boiler a small, cooked sweet rice ball as white as snow and held it to the leopard cub's mouth saying, "Come on! Here's your food. Help yourself."

But, Haqi kept crying, not bothering to smell the rice ball.

"Silly boy," said Father, as he finished the bed with the last piece of cotton batting. He then rose and took a piece of meat from a hanging cage. "Leopards are meat eaters."

He instantly frowned and said with self-reproach, "Ahh, I was being foolish myself. Haqi is too young to even eat meat soup, not to speak of meat."

His father's remark made Guoha worried. "Argh! Since he can eat neither rice nor meat, what else can he eat then?"

"He wants milk!" Father said, "He wants his mother's milk."

Guoha felt a deep pang of sorrow and turned to the cub, "Haqi, your mom…"

He stopped short of going on for fear that it might cause Haqi to grieve as well.

But, if there's no mother, where is the milk? He wondered.

Baa…baa…baa…

The bleating of a flock of goats leaked into the bamboo house.

Guoha's mother was back from grazing the goats.

Ah, the goats!

The idea dawned upon Guoha. Handing Haqi to his father, he rushed out of the bamboo house.

Without taking the time to greet his mother, Guoha dashed into the flock of goats, got hold of a big nanny goat by its curved horns, and worked hard to drag it into the bamboo house.

"What're you up to, Guoha?" asked his mother.

"Haqi is hungry for milk."

Mother looked at Guoha confounded.

Sure, he could drink milk! Guoha had learned from his mother that when he was a baby, she did not have enough milk to breastfeed him. She had to bring him up with goat milk. "If I could drink goat milk as a baby, why can't Haqi?"

Having dragged the big nanny goat into the bamboo house, he carried Haqi over and snuggled it beneath the goat's belly.

As a new mother, the big nanny goat had breasts bulging like balloons, and they were full of milk.

As if in a fairytale, Haqi began to suckle the nanny goat.

Initially, he took a sip and, feeling something wrong

with the taste, spat it all out.

After a while, however, driven either by hunger or the fresh odor of goat milk, he stuck his neck out to look for nipples with his cute little mouth.

Getting hold of one, he nursed slowly before starting to drink mouthfuls.

Grunting, grunting; gulping, gulping, with the nipple in his mouth, he was really enjoying himself.

"Hurrah!" Guoha exclaimed with glee. "He sure will be all right because he has a mom now!"

Bleating, the big nanny goat turned to examine the cuddling little thing.

While finding it hard to figure out what this kitty-like creature was, it could sense its extreme hunger; for it was gulping down one mouthful of its milk after another as if in one breath. Several times, milk sputtered out of its nostrils.

Any mother would be sad to see a baby starved like this.

Any mother would save a baby's life by breastfeeding it whether it was her own flesh and blood or not.

Soon, Haqi was full, his belly bulging like a small watermelon.

After grooming his cute face with his little paw, Haqi snuggled himself against the big nanny goat's stomach and went to sleep.

The flames from the fire pit filled the bamboo house with ample warmth.

Vying with each other, Guoha and Dad began to tell

Mom how they had found Haqi.

Mom said nodding, "Look at the adorable Haqi. He fell asleep as soon as he was full. He really knows how to enjoy himself."

Then, turning to the big nanny goat, she complimented it, "You curve-horned nanny are really being a good mom! Tomorrow, I'll take you to the freshest grass to graze, so you can produce more milk."

She had barely finished when the bamboo door was stormed open with a loud bang.

"Yikes!"

The whole family screeched in unison.

The goat was so scared that it crawled into a quilt.

At the door stood a majestic-looking, old leopard!

Its wide eyes were glaring like spotlights.

Complex feelings were exchanged between the humans and the beast in a fleeting moment: curiosity, suspicion, alarm, and hostility.

Indeed! Hostility has begun ever since human beings began to walk straight up, thus alienating themselves from the other creatures, and to wield wooden sticks and cast sharpened flints to strike them for survival.

For years, this hostility has intensified by constant human development of natural resources.

Today, while people of conscience have realized that they must protect wild animals from extinction with the greatest sympathy they can give, the wild animals have not stopped feeling hostile towards them at all.

Knowing that the people who had taken the leopard cub had fire guns, Old Leopard had been prepared before bursting into the bamboo house: It would take its cub back despite a bloody, life-and-death fight.

But, once it rested its eyes upon its well-fed baby snoozing peacefully in the cozy little bed by the fire pit, its thoughts flashed back to the cold, windy evening, when Guoha had taken off his only upper garment to swaddle its baby in it. Old Leopard shuddered at the memory.

It could not believe its eyes.

It could not comprehend why things were happening like this, either.

It doubted if it had misunderstood human beings altogether.

What it witnessed occurring under its nose made it to question its cognitive ability.

But, it had no time to seek out answers.

Seeing that the owners of the bamboo house were panicked by its presence, Old Leopard lost no time in rescuing its baby. It dashed toward the bed, picked its cub up with its mouth, and darted out of the bamboo house, vanishing in the banana forest. It left behind only the rustling of the banana leaves…

Everything happened in a blink of an eye.

The family finally collected themselves, only to fine the little warm bed empty. There was nothing but a shallow impression upon it.

"That was Haqi's father," Guoha's father said. "It doesn't trust us the same way we don't have any faith in it. We're always believing that it's a man eater."

Chapter 5

After Old Leopard took the leopard cub away, Guoha cried sadly.

Father sat in silence by the fire pit.

Mother gazed at the cozy little bed as she kept sighing.

That night, Guoha found it hard to go to sleep.

Listening to the wind rustling while lying on the floor bed, he was wondering: Where are you? Are you sleeping? Aren't you feeling cold...?

Before dawn the next day, Guoha heard someone at the bamboo door.

Someone was tapping at the door very gently.

Who could have come to visit so early in the morning?

Guoha rubbed his eyes and rushed himself off bed.

He had just opened the door when a close-up furry face caught him off guard.

Good heavens! It was Old Leopard.

It was Old Leopard that had scratched the door instead of a person.

It faltered for a second when it saw Guoha opening the door. It then placed at his foot a fluffy yellow ball that it had carried in its mouth.

Yikes! It was Haqi!

As soon as his body touched the floor, Haqi began to meow loudly.

Guoha knew that he was crying from hunger.

Guoha cast Old Leopard a look.

And Old Leopard looked back at him.

They read each other's mind through this silent eye conversation.

It turned out that Haqi had started crying from hunger before daybreak. At a loss what to do, the frantic Old Leopard had had no alternative but to circle around jumping and leaping. The cub was too young to eat nothing but milk, but where to get it? In despair, it thought of the snug bamboo house that Haqi and his parents called home. It also saw in its mind's eye the smiling faces reddened by the reflection of the flames in the fire pit. For its baby to survive, it had but to return to them for help.

Having made up its mind, Old Leopard brought Haqi back under the cover of the smoke-like morning fog.

"Old Leopard's brought Haqi back!"

As he exclaimed, Guoha took Haqi over and cuddled him in his arms.

"What? Haqi's back! Haqi's back!"

Both Father and Mother also cried with joy!

"Mom! Haqi's starving. Can we bring the nanny here now?"

"Sure, sure! Here it comes! Here it comes!"

With this, Mother led the big nanny goat into the bamboo house.

Haqi was so hungry that he could not wait. He immediately started nursing beneath the goat's belly.

He was suckling in such a hurry that he bumped its head against the goat's breasts from time to time so that milk squirted all over her face.

Old Leopard remained where it was.

Lying in a semiprone position on the deck outside, it alternated between patrolling the stockade with its vigilant, wide-open eyes and peeping at its suckling baby and the now acquainted family with a child through the bamboo door ajar.

Uhh, milk, baby, and human beings!

As he ruminated silently, Old Leopard came to a vague realization that he might have been wrong in hating humans. Look at this family. They love my leopard baby, treat it tenderly, feed it, and keep it alive after it lost its mother. How kind they are!

But, are all human beings this kind-hearted?

If so, how to interpret the behavior of the man who set the traps?

Old Leopard found no answers to these questions.

After turning its thoughts over and over, it came to the conclusion that human beings could not be easily trusted, and animals were not to relax their vigilance against them.

When Haqi was full, Old Leopard suddenly broke into the room and snatched him away.

Early the next evening, under the cover of the twilight, Old Leopard brought the hungry Haqi back in the same manner that he had taken Haqi away without notice. It scratched the bamboo door of Guoha's house.

The pattern of bringing Haqi back when he was hungry and took him away after he was fed was repeated for the next four or five days.

How Guoha and his parents wished that Old Leopard would have left Guoha in their care instead of moving him to and fro.

But, how could they communicate with Old Leopard?

And, coming back and forth, Old Leopard had no intention to sit down for the communication whatsoever.

But, Old Leopard changed its mind on the morning of the seventh day.

It indicated that it would like to have a talk with Guoha's family.

This time, it lay down silently by the fire pit instead of taking cover on the deck. Its eyes ping-ponged from its suckling baby to every member of the family.

Yes, what a happy family it was!

Old Leopard had had a happy family like it.

How delighted the leopard couple had been with the birth of their leopard cub.

Even before their baby had opened its eyes, they had been planning to take it for a walk in the forest on a beautiful sunny day.

They had meant to teach him to climb, to swim, to turn sharply while sprinting, to prance over an obstacle during a fast chase, and hide by blending itself with the surroundings in case of an emergency.

They had also thought of teaching it to identify the various marks left by different animals and to decode the body language they would use to communicate with it, such as snorting, tail wagging, and paw lifting.

In a word, they had wanted to teach their cub everything a true leopard was supposed to know and do. They had meant to correct the mistakes that it might have made through continuous training so that it would have matured day by day.

The leopard couple had imagined taking their cub to the intoxicating evening party that every leopard had yearned for. They had wanted him to see the world and to get acquainted with his fellow leopards gathering from all parts of the big forest.

How mysterious the evening party had been!

Solitary leopards from near and far leave their home ranges to get together in an agreed-upon place in the forest every other few days. They do so to maintain the stability of a leap, or a large family, of leopards. They sit around gazing at each other as a form of extending their greetings. Sometimes, a few naughty leopards frolic with each other for a while, which can be seen as an awesome performance. After sharing their current situation in particular and reviewing the stability and prosperity of the leap at large, they disperse, each returning to its respective territory.

The Old Leopard couple had thought their cub would have been liked and praised by everyone at the party. Maybe it would have performed a few marvelous stunts like prancing and spinning to win everyone's applause!

But now…

As if he had known how sad Old Leopard was secretly feeling, Guoha looked up and said to it,

"Look! Old Leopard, isn't Haqi doing well? See how he's enjoying the milk. Well, you may not know that Haqi is what we call your baby. We've named him for you."

Gazing at Guoha, Old Leopard appeared to be an attentive listener.

"Well, I'd like to tell you that 'qi' means 'one family.'" Father cut in, "Your baby is now a member of our family. We will take good care of him. Please leave him to us. It would be stressful to the baby to be hauled back and forth every day. Besides, even a lamb suckles several times a day. Haqi would be starving if you let him drink only twice."

Old Leopard blinked its big eyes, as if to indicate its comprehension of what Father had said.

However, it had not made up its mind whether to leave Haqi with the family or not.

After all, Mother was the most empathetic to what Old Leopard was feeling. She said, "I know you hate to part with your baby. It's true that no parents like to be separated from their children. How about leaving Haqi to the care of a surrogate goat mother and picking him up after he's weened. Then, we'll return him to you for good. What do you think?"

After she finished, Mother gazed into Old Leopard's eyes.

Old Leopard blinked.

It hung its head down and remained silent for a moment. It then rose slowly from beside the fire pit.

It walked up to Haqi, dropped a few tender kisses on his cheeks, and gave his fine coat a few soft licks. Then, it looked up and surveyed everyone by the fire pit with a trustful look. It seemed to say either "Bye!" or "Thanks, you kind-hearted humans!"

Just then, Haqi burst into a loud cry, "Meow!"

Haqi had recognized the odor of his father who had groomed him. He seemed to have realized that his father was going to leave him.

His screech rent the hearts of both Old Leopard and Guoha's family.

Guoha and his parents watched Old Leopard silently.

Glancing back at Guoha, Old Leopard left without hesitation.

Neither footfalls nor rustles of banana leaves were heard in its wake.

Old Leopard left its cub behind in this silent manner.

Seeing it turning around and stepping out of the bamboo house, Guoha had suddenly felt a sense of loss, as if he had had a lot to tell Old Leopard. He rushed out.

But, Old Leopard was gone.

Only the banana trees stood soundless down the stilted bamboo house.

Guoha said to himself:

Old Leopard, don't worry! Remember to pick Haqi up when he's a grownup.

Chapter 6

Old Leopard trotted out of the stockade via a remote path under the cover of the fog.

When am I going to pick up my baby?

Old Leopard was pondering.

Yep, wait till he's weaned.

It'll live a happy life in the care of the kind family.

As he was thinking and walking, Old Leopard looked up at the grayish morning sky and let out a heavy sigh of relief.

In the twilit sky, there floated a white cloud.

Old Leopard stopped to gaze at it.

It suddenly realized that the shape of the cloud resembled the face of its spouse.

Hey, you're not at rest?

You're still watching us?

I know you're worrying about our baby and me as well.

So thinking, Old Leopard said to the cloud in silence, "You gave up your life trying to protect our baby. Now that he is entrusted to the kind, trustworthy family of Guoha, you may rest in peace."

The cloud was drifting south wordlessly.

It drifted until it vanished in the grayish morning sky. Old leopard lowered its head.

Both my wife and son have found their homes, he thought. What about me?

Suddenly, Old Leopard shook its golden fur coat, and it shook himself out of the fleeting reverie. Then, perking up its head, it marched toward the Motagu Forest...

I must embrace the new day in earnest and pass it with courage and wisdom, Old Leopard told itself.

It arrived under a soap-bean tree, by which it had passed daily to sneak into the stockade. There, he spotted a carcass of a rabbit, seemingly dropped by an absent-minded hunter.

Old Leopard had never felt so tired and hungry since he became a father.

Indeed. He had been playing the roles of both a father and a mother in the past few days.

The rabbit could serve as a perfect breakfast.

Old Leopard would have never gobbled up a rabbit of an unknown origin unless it was extremely hungry and overexcited over the babysitting solution.

It had barely walked a few steps after the breakfast when it was hit by an excruciating abdominal pain, so much so that it felt a knife were being twisted in its entrails.

Ouch!

Old Leopard could not help crying out and dropped to the ground writhing in agony.

This was the first time that it had given way to pain to the best of its memory.

Old Leopard was poisoned.

The rabbit was poisonous.

It knew it by instinct.

Now, it recalled what its father had told it when it was young: Human urine could be used as an antidote.

It had to find it despite its pain.

It would be its lifesaver.

Ahh, human urine! Human beings!

Old Leopard struggled up and glanced back toward the stockade enshrouded in fog.

It seemed to see Guoha and his parents waving at it on their deck.

It turned around and walked toward the stockade and Guoha's home.

But, it had taken only a few steps when it collapsed gasping for air.

The stockade was too far away. So was Guoha's house. No way, he thought, I can never make it…

It sighed heavily, unable to keep its eyelids from falling shut.

Just then, a peculiar odor was carried over by a cold breeze and gave the drowsed Old Leopard a shudder.

Ah, it was human urine!

Old Leopard opened its eyes wide and trained them toward the source of the odor.

It spotted an earthen jar hanging from a branch of a soapbean tree not high above the ground.

The odor of the human urine came from the jar.

What's going on?

Who's hung his urine over a tree fork?

Why has a jar of human urine suddenly appeared on a fork when I'm in dire need of it?

Old Leopard did not have time to mull over its own questions because the only thing on its mind was to leap up and grab the jar. It gazed at it, its eyes reddened by the poison.

It was thinking that by getting hold of the jar, it would be able to live on and take its cub back to the forest to do what a father was supposed to do: teaching it to survive tenaciously so that their leopard leap could multiply indefinitely...

Old Leopard dragged its body to under the soap-bean tree.

It knew that with its remaining physical strength, it was impossible to climb to the tree to reach the earthen jar.

However, the desire for survival urged it to muster up all the strength it had and darted into the air extending its paws as far as possible to grab the jar.

It was confident that it would never miss it.

It could have reached this height by an effortless leap before.

But, when it landed, it found its paws empty.

It had missed the jar by only a fraction of an inch.

It struggled to fight back the harrowing pain, its widened eyes spitting fire at the jar hanging over the fork.

It was going to leap again.

It was going to exert all its efforts to embrace survival.

Not only for itself but also for its son.

With a roar, it sprang into the air.

It figured that leapt higher than it had previously attempted.

And that it could get hold of the jar with no question.

However, the ruthless reality dealt it a cruel blow:

It had leapt even lower.

It had failed to get the jar once again.

No, I must keep jumping, he thought.

It wanted to jump a third time.

It wanted to jump a fourth or even a fifth time.

But, it could no longer do so.

Old Leopard was now so exhausted that it did not even had the strength to keep its head up.

It widened its nostrils to take in the odor of human urine permeating the air around...

The odor of life was beckoning.

It panted out mouthfuls of hot breaths in order to gasp in more cool air to soothe the pain in its stomach. It was summoning every ounce of strength that he had to make a last attempt, an attempt that would determine his life or death.

It was about to make its final leap when suddenly a face flashed like an aspiration in a bush nearby.

A human face!

Old Leopard caught a clear sight of the fleeting face: It was indeed a human face, a face it had never seen before; a face filled with unchecked fear, savage, and greed, and a disfigured by the success of a scheme.

In a breath of time, Old Leopard realized that it had fallen into a trap.

A trap set by a vicious human being.

It was a man who wanted to make a fortune by getting his hands on a precious leopard skin and more valuable leopard bones to be used as an ingredient of traditional medicine. He had put down the poisonous rabbit on the trail that he had found Old Leopard laying while taking its cub to the stockade back and forth. He had also hung the earthen jar over the tree fork to tantalize his victim so that its frequent jumps would accelerate the process of poisoning and its death. Besides, he had meant for his victim to die where it was instead of running into the forest due to its pain so that he could get his windfall hands down.

What a mean and atrocious man he was!

Not only did he put down the poison, but he also set the trap to speed up his victim's demise while it was leaping desperately to reach the antidote. And he would go so far as to watch cold-heartedly in hiding the unfolding of the tragedy of its victim dying sooner of its desire for survival.

What an insidious and cold-blooded man!

Roooaaarrr!

Old Leopard's outcry shook leaves off from the soap-bean tree.

It felt that it roared the loudest in its entire life.

Whoosh!

Old Leopard sprang up and pounced toward the bushes like a whirlwind whipping up a cloud of dust.

It had not expected that, while still shivering from pain, it should have had such explosive strength.

If it had had such strength, it would have broken a fork, not to mention grabbing the jar.

The man hiding in the bushes had not imagined that a

poisoned old leopard should have been able to launch such a fierce attack.

He had had time neither to run nor cry before his neck was broken by the Old Leopard with a single strike of its paw.

He fell in a pool of blood with his shattered dream of making a fortune.

Old Leopard shivered all over again, not knowing if it was because of the intensifying cramps in his stomach or because of the trauma of killing a human being for the first time in its entire life.

It shifted its eyes to the stockade from the viciously looking man lying in the blood.

In its mind's eye, it saw Guoha's family sitting around the fire pit in the cozy bam-boo house.

Alas! Humans!

While they are all humans, why are there such big differences between them?

Do they have different hearts?

But why? And why are some humans soft-hearted and others hard-hearted?

In its dying moment, Old Leopard kept asking itself the same questions and giving itself the affirmative and negative answers alternately.

Old Leopard collapsed with the physical abdominal pain and the more intense mental agony in its search for answers.

It was already feeling its nonexistence in this world.

The otherwise brightening Morning Star appeared darker and darker in its eyes.

It could not figure out why the sky got darker as the day was breaking.

It struggled to raise its head and uttered its last, depressing call toward the stockade where cooking smoke was rising and toward the morning sky that was turning from gray to darkness:

Alas! Humans, be kind!

Be compassionate and spare my son!

Part II

Haqi, Where Are You?

Chapter 7

Haqi grew up day by day.

He opened his eyes and saw Guoha's family attending him.

He pricked his ears and heard Guoha and his parents talking and laughing.

Seeing the bed in the bamboo house too small for Haqi to sleep in, Father crafted a big one with straw and placed it on the deck.

During the day, Haqi would lie on the deck guarding the house in earnest while Guoha's family were working away from home.

In the evening, he would, meowing with great joy, leap off the deck to greet Guoha and his parents returning with their flock of goats.

He could pick his goat mother out of the flock at a glance.

He would dash over and tenderly lick her legs and nasal bridge with the tip of his tongue.

The nanny goat would lick her surrogate son back while telling him in a whispering bleat how much she had missed him when she had been away.

After supper, each member of Guoha's family began to mind his or her own business.

As soon as Guoha set about doing his homework, Haqi went and took him his small bamboo stool in his mouth.

When he saw Mother getting ready for her needlework, Haqi carried in his mouth her bamboo basket used as a sewing kit.

While Father was splitting firewood in the courtyard, Haqi jumped here and there to pick up the scattered pieces and heap them up.

Seeing Father wipe sweat off his face with the front of his shirt, Haqi rushed into the bamboo house and picked up a towel for him.

Night fell, and wind sprang up.

The bamboo door squeaked as the wind tugged it to and fro.

Haqi pulled himself up and lay down against the door to keep it shut so that it would no longer disturb his sleeping family members.

One day, Guoha had been caught in the rain on his way back from school. Once he was home, Mother changed his clothes instantly. Meanwhile, Haqi stood up and, placing his front paws on his shoulders, licked his hair dry bit by bit.

Growing increasingly thoughtful, Haqi became an inseparable member of Guoha's family.

But, when Guoha came back from school one evening, he found Haqi absent from the deck.

At first, Guoha thought that Haqi might be playing hide-and-seek with him. He rushed into the bamboo house to look for him, only to see him not there. He then searched in the yard but still failed to locate him.

Guoha grew worried.

Mom and dad are still working in the fields. Where can Haqi be? Guoha wondered.

He lies on the deck to wait for us to come home every day.

While Guoha was tortured by his anxiety, Uncle Tezhang, a blacksmith from the same stockade, came.

"Guoha, I saw your Haqi ran into the woods in the south."

"Really? Are you sure?"

Now, Guoha became more concerned.

He was worrying that Haqi might get lost or, even worse, get hurt in an accident.

Without waiting for his parents to return, he dashed into the woods himself.

He called as he walked in the forest, wishing that Haqi would suddenly pop up in front of him.

Unfortunately, Guoha still failed to find Haqi even when he had shouted himself hoarse and become both hungry and exhausted.

Night gradually set in, and Guoha felt as if he was groping in a humongous iron pot turned upside down. He could see nothing but darkness.

Owls were hooting horrifyingly above him.

And wolves were howling dolefully in the distance.

Guoha was scared.

He fumbled to get back home but could not find his way out of the woods any more.

Guoha got lost.

Sleepiness and hunger attacked alternately.

He walked and walked when his knees buckled, and he fell under a tree.

He tried to push his body up with his arms, but they felt so feeble that they were out of his control.

His eyelids grew so heavy that he fell asleep instantly under the tree.

In his sleep, he had a nightmare. He dreamed of Haqi falling into a swamp, and when he rushed over trying to pull him out, he, too, fell into the fathomless quagmire…

Ruff, ruff, ruff!

Wuff, wuff, wuff!

The yelps woke him up with a startle.

He opened his eyes and found, to his astonishment, that he had fallen asleep under a big tree.

A few steps away stood a ring of dogs barking at him wildly.

Guoha recognized them. They are the dogs from his stockade.

Strangely, they stood in a circle orderly. None, however, would dare to venture up, as if someone had drawn an impenetrable circular barrier in front of them.

Guoha quickly pulled himself up from the ground.

He caught sight of many flickering pine torches in the dark woods.

The torches were closing from all directions.

"Guoha…"

"Guoha…"

As torches were drawing near, people's calls began to be audible.

People from my stockade are looking for me! He thought.

"Hey, I am here!" Guoha shouted back with joy.

The people looking for Guoha were quickly closing in.

In the brightly dancing flame of the torches, Guoha spotted Father and Uncle Tezhang leading the crowd.

Father and Uncle Tezhang had just entered the "dog ring" when a leopard whooshed down from the tree. Pitching itself between Guoha and the approaching duo, it roared fiercely at them. Its head held high and its hair standing on end, it was ready for a desperate fight.

Guoha took a closer look and, to his amazement, found it to be Haqi.

Meanwhile, Haqi and Father also recognized each other.

"Haqi!" The father and son called with happy surprise and, rushing over together, gave him a big hug.

Father and Mother felt enormous relief at locating both Guoha and Haqi at the same time.

Guoha had a lot of questions for Haqi, but how could Haqi tell him?

So, he had to turn to his father for an answer, "Dad, why did Haqi run into the woods?"

Pressing some tobacco into a huge bamboo water pipe, Father said, a fledgling cuckoo chick must learn to fly. Growing up day by day, Haqi wants to support himself."

Ahh! Guoha now realized that Haqi had been to the woods to look for food.

As Father smoked with great content, his water pipe gurgled and gurgled. Then he slowly puffed out a misty cloud of smoke.

"By nature," he began, "leopards are nocturnal animals. They sleep during the day and hunt during the night. This is the first time Haqi's trying to hunt at night. He couldn't wait for us to get back before sneaking into the woods in the evening. He'll spend the whole night there learning the skills of hunting. So, from now on, our Haqi is going to earn his own living."

Guoha asked with concern, "What if he gets lost and

can't find his way home?"

"Haha," Father broke into a laughter. "It was you who couldn't get back home the other day, but Haqi can. Animals' instinct is far superior to humans'. No matter how far he wanders, he will always leave his mark along his way, say, by peeping or rubbing himself on trees. He will then snuff his way back with his sharp nose, and he'll never get lost. You wondered why those dogs didn't dare to approach you but instead only yelped around you from a distance, didn't you?"

"Yah!" Guoha nodded and asked, "Why then?"

"That was because Haqi had left his mark, and it prevented them from getting close to you."

Puffing his water pipe, Father said deliberately, "When you went to look for Haqi in the woods, you got lost instead of finding him and fell asleep under a tree. Haqi located you by picking up your odor. When he saw you snoozing, he didn't wake you up because he wanted you to have a good sleep. There were many wild animals in the woods. To prevent them from harming you, he peed around you. His pee smelt so strong that no animal dared to come near you. Dogs fear leopards the most. That was why they didn't dare to reach you. Still concerned, Haqi leapt up to the tree and guarded you from there. He would have pounced upon anyone who would take the risk of breaking through the circle of his urine. In case of being no match for his opponent, he would have dragged you to the tree and hidden you up there. He would have given up anything to stop anyone from harming you. Didn't you see him pounce at me and Uncle Tezhang from the tree when we were stepping into the circle of his pee? He hadn't recognized us at the beginning because of the overpowering scent of the pine torches. His fierce look was pretty scary, wasn't it? Well, if he had not figured out who we were, he would have given us a terrible bite."

Then, Father looked up. Gazing at Haqi resting on the deck, he continued tenderly, "This orphaned leopard is deeply bounded to us, particularly to you. Guoha, you two play together and eat the good food fixed by your mom together. You groom him when he sleeps on the deck and ride on his back when you swim in the pond. Treating you closer than a biological brother, He would rick his life for the safety of yours if anyone should have the guts to hurt you."

Father's words struck a deep chord in Guoha's heart.

He said to himself, I, too, would give up my life to protect Haqi from any harm.

Time went by so quickly that, in a blink of an eye, the banana sucker by the bamboo house had grown into a big plant. The kitty-like leopard cub had also matured into a real leopard like his father. As strong as a pony, he had a glistening gold coat with beautiful patterns of black rings on it, the distinctively contrasting black and yellow colors making the coat even more dazzling. He also boasted a gorgeous long tail and stuck it up proudly whenever he was on the run. Seen from a distance, it appeared like a glistening golden rod. Haqi's big eyes, reminiscent of his father, always shone like spotlights. His ever-bristling long whiskers added to his majestic look.

However, with his growth, Haqi began to get himself into constant trouble.

Chapter 8

The goats and cattle in the stockade were the first to feel threatened by Haqi's growth into adulthood.

When evening came, the goats and cattle, having grazed to their fill, returned to the stockade, humming their somewhat syncopated ditties to the accompaniment of the jingling bells hanging from their necks. They were approaching the entrance when they ran into Haqi exiting the stockade to go on his hunting trip. The faint-hearted goats immediately huddled into a solid mass, struggling with one another as they flinched and bleated in alarm. Some

were so scared that they turned around and scampered away, afraid to return to their pens. Meanwhile, the cattle stared at Haqi in a row with their widened eyes and aimed their horns at him while mooing at the top of their lungs.

Whenever this happened, Haqi would remain where he was in silence, meaning to let the goats and cattle into the stockade.

However, the goats and cattle would mistake Haqi's stance as making a choice to see which of them would best fit his supper.

They would be deadlocked and block the entrance to the stockade.

Then, if the flock of Guoha's family happened to arrive, the stalemate would be broken with ease.

The nanny goat would come up to Guoha, lick his forehead and nasal bridge as she had done when she breastfed him as a baby. Haqi would lick back at his goat mother's chest and neck. After they exchanged their physical affection, the nanny goat would stand in front of Haqi, turn to the dumbfounded goats and cattle, and gave a couple of loud bleats. The animals would then collect themselves as if waking from a dream and, vying with one another, crowd into the gate of the stockade.

During the midnight, when Haqi returned from hunting and sauntered into the stockade in the bright moonlight, his glowing eyes, as well as his aggressive and unnerving odor, would create a tremendous commotion among the goats and cattle in their pens. The riot would cause their owners to hurry into their pants and rush out to check, kerosene lantern in one hand and pant waist in the other.

After they figured out what was going on, they would certainly curse Haqi. Some of them would also put the blame on Guoha and his parents, saying "Well, it's like a duck trying to bark. Why are they raising a leopard at home to keep us on tenterhooks while there are other animals they can care for?"

As a Hani proverb goes, "A cold stone can be warmed if held to the bosom long enough," the villagers, old and young, became accustomed to Haqi as time went by.

Knowing that he was a harmless beast of prey, they no longer feared him. Some even brought food to him from time to time.

But, unprepared strangers who passed by to ask for thirst-quenching water would be startled and take to their heels in panic.

Eventually, Haqi got himself into trouble.

One day, Uncle Tezhang's cousin Asha came to visit him from afar.

Dressed in her best and carrying a jar of high-quality honey, she was beside herself with joy.

She was reaching the stockade when Haqi bumped into her.

"Aah!"

How could Asha, who was innately timid, withstand such a chance meeting!

With a screech, her legs went, and she collapsed to the ground with a thump.

Her head and face were covered with the high-quality honey from the jar.

Assuming that Haqi was charging at her, she screamed at the top of her voice, "Help! Help!"

She rolled about on the ground crying out loud.

Meanwhile, Haqi gazed at her attentively.

Haqi was wondering why this woman tossing herself on the ground and whether she could rise again.

To lend her a helping paw, he went up to her. Holding her by her sleeves in his mouth, he dragged her hard, attempting to pull her up.

His move horrified Asha even more.

"The leopard's biting me! The leopard's eating me!"

Her screams shook the entire stockade up.

Tezhang dashed out of his house and caught sight of Haqi engaging his cousin. He picked up a wooden stick and charged at Haqi.

Haqi, however, thought that the stick would fall upon the woman on the ground.

He could not understand why the man should hit the woman who was already fallen.

He felt obliged to protect the weaker party.

Turning his head abruptly, he took hold of the wrist part of Tezhang's hand holding the stick.

Tezhang squawked with sharp pain and dropped the stick.

After letting Tezhang's wrist go, Haqi was still snarling.

Shielding the woman on the ground, he refused to allow Tezhang move an inch toward her.

In the end, it was Guoha's father who rushed over to intervene and get the two out of the predicament.

Haqi had left some fairly deep bite marks in Tezhang's wrist. It took several days for them to heal after being bandaged with some herbal ointment. Asha had hemmed herself in with her squash-like swollen face stung by the bees attracted by the honey plastered on it. Frightened out of her senses, she had been raving in her delirium for days.

Later, Tezhang's wife, well-known to her fellow villagers for being willful and unreasonable, stormed into Guoha's house to harass the family. She insisted that Guoha and his parents send Haqi away. Otherwise, she threatened, she would kill Haqi with her shotgun.

"Then, don't you blame me for being too harsh on you!" She continued, "We may be good neighbors for years and somewhat related in the blood line, but you can't just say something apologetic and keep this man-biting leopard."

Guoha was angry and could not help retorting her, saying, "Haqi never bites anyone. He would have never bitten Uncle Tezhang if he had not tried to hit him with a stick."

"What? How can you blame the fish when you are choked by a fish bone?" Pointing her sharp-nailed fingers at Guoha's forehead as if to drill a hole in it, Tezhang's wife went on fuming, "It doesn't bite people? It doesn't bite anyone? What do you mean by biting people? Do you mean by biting off a person's head? Hold out your hand and take a bite from me, and see if you'll feel the pain!"

She harangued continuously until she finally annoyed Haqi, who had been napping on the deck. He stood up and roared at her, which sent her scrambling away trembling. As she was fleeing, she nimbly picked up the pair of beautiful silver bracelets from the bamboo table.

The bracelets belonged to Guoha's mother, who had taken them off and placed them on the table when she set out dying her coarse cloth with indigo that could have corroded the jewelry.

In fact, upon entering the house, Tezheng's wife had noticed the bracelets that she had long been coveting.

"Well, it's up to you to shoot or not to shoot and kill Haqi. I will sell the bracelets for the tonic to help Tezhang heal his wound. But, I must warn you first: If the tonic doesn't work, I'll sure come back to take more stuff. You must remember that Tezhang is the only bread-earner in our family."

As she grumbled, she slipped away as fast as if her heels were lubricated.

Chapter 9

With the silver bracelets taken away, Guoha and his parents thought that this would be the end of the trouble. But, the next day, Guoha found, to his surprise, Haqi limping back from hunting.

"Dad, Haqi is hurt!"

"What?" Father dashed out of the bamboo house and asked, "Really?"

Haqi had been wounded; he had been shot by a gun. His wounded hind leg was covered with dried blood, trembling with pain.

Nevertheless, he appeared not to be painful at all. He rubbed his face on Father's legs and licked Guoha's palm as affectionately as he always did after returning home.

It was apparent that he had deliberately licked the blood off his wound lest his loved ones notice his injury and feel sad.

To Haqi's innocent mind, he had gotten his hind leg pricked by something that he had accidently stepped on and popped mysteriously. He had never expected that he should have been hurt by humans.

Seeing Haqi trying hard to mask his pain with a pretense that nothing had happened, Guoha felt a pang of mental agony. So much so that he could hardly hold back his tears. He complimented Haqi, "You, you are really awesome…"

"Phew! He was lucky! His bone was intact." Father gave a big sigh of relief after examining Haqi carefully. "It would be bad if his bone had been damaged."

"Could it be Uncle Tezhang who shot him?" asked Guoha angrily after drying his teary eyes. "Isn't it enough to take away the bracelets? Why would he be so revengeful as to hurt Haqi?"

Father shook his head, "No, your Uncle Tezhang is not that kind of a person."

Father fetched some herbal medicine and was about to rub it on Haqi's wound after rinsing it.

"Yikes!" Father suddenly exclaimed, "The iron pellets!"

He removed two pellets from the messy tissues under the skin around the wound.

Instead of being round, the blood-stained pellets were three-edged.

"None of us in the stockade use this kind of pellet."

Gazing at the edged pellets held on Father's palm, Guoha said, "This confirms that Uncle Tezhang did not shoot Haqi."

As soon as Guoha finished, a voice boomed from under the stilted bamboo house, "Your Uncle Tezhang is not as mean as you thought."

The voice came from none other than Uncle Tezhang.

"Haha! Talking of the devil, the devil comes!" Father laughed.

Guoha also beamed and said, "Uncle Tezhang, I wronged you. I must apologize!"

"It's okay! It's okay! You didn't wrong me at all. If I had not wielded the stick, Haqi would not have bitten me. I deserved it."

Then, he made to the deck unhurriedly while producing the silver bracelets from within the fronts of his upper garment. He said, "I'm here to see Haqi. I was worried when I learned that he had been hurt by someone. Besides, I'm here to return the silver bracelets. That notorious wife of mine, if she did anything wrong, I'd like to apologize on her behalf."

With this, Uncle Tezhang handed the bracelets to Father and then stroked Haqi's forehead tenderly.

Father asked with concern, "How's your wrist? Is it still hurting?"

Uncle Tezhang shook his head and said, "It's been healed already. Everyone says leopards' teeth are poisonous, and a bite would be deadly. Now, it seems to be a tall tale."

Father asked again, "How's your cousin? I'm sorry for what had happened to her!"

"Well, there's nothing to be sorry about. She has a lily liver as small as the eye of a needle. I've figured it all out: Haqi didn't bite her. She collapsed to the ground merely out of fear. Haqi did hold her by her sleeve, but he was trying to pull her up. Of course, she'd never seen Haqi before and took it for granted that he was going to bite her. Haha! When I was passing by the entrance of our stockade a moment ago, I saw a crowd of people around there. It was said that they were from another stockade over the mountain and had come here to avenge me. They had had hearsay that Haqi had killed both me and my cousin. See what the blasted bad mouths have done! They've spread the rumor like mad, from one person to ten, and then from ten to a hundred. Within a couple days, they've turned a flea into an elephant."

Uncle Tezhang burst into a guffaw after he finished.

Then, he asked Father, "How about Haqi's wound? Did any of his bones get hurt?"

"Luckily, his bones are intact."

"As an old saying goes, 'it takes a hundred days to heal an injured bone.' Who did it?"

"Take a look at these and you'll know," said Father as he handed the two iron pellets over.

Uncle Tezhang took the pellets. As soon as he glanced at them, he pulled his bushy eyebrows together. He said, "Only those from the Manzhe Stockade use this kind of three-edged pellets."

Hearing this, Guoha gave a shudder, "Is that the stockade that poisoned Old Leopard to death?"

Uncle Tezhang nodded.

Father also furrowed his brows and said, "As a tree has its root, so water has its source. Haqi's father killed the person who had put down the poison, and now, they are here to have Haqi pay with his life."

"When a mountain torrent rises, we must build our dam. Since some people are bent on killing Haqi, we must be vigilant. They may have failed today, but they will not take it lying down. Perhaps, they'll give it another try tomorrow. Besides, always going in and out of places full of people, Haqi risks being killed by a reckless person as a man-eating beast sooner or later." Shaking his head, Uncle Tezhang continued, "Haqi didn't hurt anyone, but they lie about him and try to take his life. This is outrageous. There'd been such a fine family of leopards, and now only Haqi's survived. We can't let anything bad happen to him again!"

Looking into Tezhang's eyes, Father questioned, "Bro, do you have a good idea?"

"Well, I've got this: Since his leg is wounded, I'll make an iron chain so that you can lock him up and let him recover from his injury at home. Even after he gets back on feet, chain him home as a domestic animal. Let's work ourselves harder to hunt food for him."

In the evening, Uncle Tezhang brought a chain over as he had promised.

A long, clanking, big iron chain.

Haqi had never seen an iron chain before. Rising from the deck, he came over to look and sniff at it with curiosity.

What is it used for? He wondered.

But, he had no idea.

Only when Father picked the chain up and was about to put it over his neck did Haqi realize its application.

He growled anxiously.

Seizing a chance, he suddenly threw himself to the ground from the stilted bamboo house.

The newly bandaged wound gave him a sharp pain. He limped and stumbled.

But, he managed to stand; only that he kept his wounded leg half-lifted in the air, shivering from pain.

He would rather looked back at Haqi and his father up on the deck than run away.

His widened eyes were filled with question marks.

Why are you trying to chain me up? He asked silently.

Have I done anything wrong?

Seeing the pain in Haqi's eyes, Guoha felt as agonized as if a knife were being twisted in his heart.

Holding his father with both his arms, he entreated,

"Dad, don't chain him! Don't chain him up! He's used to running out to hunt. He would be bored to death in chains."

Father sighed helplessly and said, "We have to. Otherwise, when he went out to look for food...."

"When he goes out, I will tag along and stay close to him." Guoha cut his father short and begged hard, "Dad, please! Don't worry! I'll protect him. Please don't chain him up! Please! I am begging you, dad!"

"My silly son!" said Father with tensed muscles on his cheeks, letting the chain slip from his hand and drop clanking on the deck.

He sat down, picked up the big bamboo water pipe, and began smoking it. He smoked so hard that the pipe burbled and gurgled while the bulging veins on his forehead were throbbing like wriggling earthworms.

After a while, he laid down the pipe and said to Guoha, "It's so late, and your mom isn't back yet. When she was leaving this morning, she told me that the big nanny was going to have kids. Hurry to the mountain and take a look."

With an "okay," Guoha trotted out of the stockade.

He had just cantered for a short distance when he ran into his mother herding the family's goats back.

He asked his mother, "Has the nanny goat given birth to her kids?"

The puzzled mother shook her head, "There's no such thing!"

"What? There's no such thing?"

His heart skipped a beat. Suddenly, something dawned upon him, and he turned and darted home.

But it was too late.

The chain was already around Haqi's neck.

"Haqi! Haqi!"

Guoha shouted and rushed up the deck toward Haqi with his arms held out.

Clanking! Clanking!

Haqi growled.

"Haqi! Haqi! Dad shouldn't have lied to me. He shouldn't have chained you up!"

Holding Haqi's neck in his arms, Guoha burst into tears.

Clanking! Clanking!

Haqi gently licked the tears off Guoha's face with the tip of his tongue as the thick chain clanked and clanked...

Chapter 10

Tonight, the moon was always hiding behind the clouds.

The faint moonlight shrouded the mountains like a thin veil of dusty smoke.

The distant mountain seemed like an irregularly cut piece of cloth pasted on the vault of heaven. The nearby banana grove and the wild papaya trees looked vague and shapeless.

Despite the extra thick layer of straw that Father had added to his bed, Haqi found it hard to fall asleep.

Indeed! He would normally have been leaping about freely in the woods.

But, tonight, he was fettered to the deck.

He looked up at the evening sky.

It was not bright because the moon remained unseen behind the clouds.

Why is the moon doing so? He wondered.

Why doesn't it break out of the clouds and pour all its light onto the ground at will?

What does the moon fear?

Is it afraid of being chained up, too?

If so, it can't go anywhere, just like me…

Sticking out his tongue, Haqi licked the chain around his neck.

The chain felt icy.

He tried tugging it, and it clanked. The chain was fastened firmly to a column of the house.

So, am I going to be chained like this all the time? He thought.

Am I going to spend the rest of my life being fed by people in chains?

Is this poor little area on the deck within the circumference defined by the length of the chain going to be my sphere of life while I could have roamed on the endless expanse of the land?

A nocturnal bird flew twittering by from the remote distance in the sky high above. Fluttering freely, it disappeared like a dart.

It could fly wherever it desired.

Because it was free.

Then, there came a series of bleating from the shadowy distant mountain.

Brrrr-brrrrr!

Those were the care-free cry of red deer.

They must have been drinking at the little pond with salty water in the gully or looking for a grove of trees with young leaves unfurling on them.

They could go wherever they wanted.

Because they were free.

But, why did kind-hearted Father first hid the chain, coaxed me up to the deck of the bamboo house, and then suddenly put the chain around my neck?

No matter how painfully I struggled, he wouldn't relent and instead forced me to give in by grabbing my injured leg forcefully. Doesn't he know that I want to be an unrestrained bird that enjoys the freedom of flying high and low?

Doesn't he know that I want to be an unfettered deer that enjoys the freedom of leaping here and there?

Haqi groaned inwardly not only because of his loss of freedom but also because of his first rift with Father, and what was worse, the rift was irreconcilable.

Having weighed the alternatives carefully in his mind,

he finally made his decision.

He was going to break the chain with his teeth.

He was going to set himself free.

In order not to make a sound to disturb the people in the bamboo house, Haqi held the chain with his front paws and, turning his head sideways, tried biting it with one tooth at a time.

He wanted to find the strongest tooth to deal with this object imbued with the scent of iron and carbon.

Clanking! Clanking!

Although he exercised extreme caution to minimize the clanking, the little sound he made was still clearly audible in the silence of the midnight.

He had but to pause from time to time and looked back at the unlit bamboo house where the flame in the fire pit had long been smothered.

The bamboo house was very quiet.

I'm so lucky that Guoha and his parents are fast asleep now, he thought.

In reality, they were not.

How could they go to sleep?

Guoha heard the chain clanking, each clank tugging at one of his heartstrings.

He nudged awake his father sleeping on his left side and said, "Dad! Dad! Listen! Haqi is trying to break the chain with his teeth."

Father did not budge.

Guoha thought him to be slumbering.

He then gently pushed his mother on the right and said, "Mom! Mom! Listen. Haqi can't take it. He's biting the chain!"

Mother remained silent.

Guoha deemed that his mother was also snoozing.

He was frantic, tossing and turning in bed.

Now, he took comfort in thinking: Haqi. Go ahead and bite the chain off. Tomorrow, I will make sure that Dad won't put it back around your neck.

Then, he pondered with concern: Haqi, stop biting the chain. How can you break it? It's made from iron, and it will damage your teeth.

Indeed, how could Haqi break the iron chain forged by Uncle Tezhang who had been an ironsmith for more than forty years?

Haqi worked on the chain for the better part of the night until his gum was bleeding. When he looked down at the chain, he found only a few scratches left by his teeth.

The tooth marks were so shallow that they were even able to reflect the moonlight.

Haqi was frustrated.

He resented toughness of the chain.

He hated the softness of his teeth.

He held his head up and uttered a muffled, heartbroken moan at the moon behind the clouds.

Mooooaaaannn…

After that, he resumed working on the chain.

He kept biting and moaning alternately.

Each moan sounded hoarser and hoarser.

Each cry became more and more desperate.

Mooooaaaannn…!

The raspy lament was like a pair of scissors breaking the hearts of Guoha and his parents to pieces.

They could no long bear it.

Suddenly, they heard different sounds of crying and biting mixed into those of Haqi's.

Haqi and his parents sprang up from their floor bed almost simultaneously.

They were alarmed when they opened the door…

In the faint, misty moonlight, poor Haqi, coiling himself into a bundle and holding the chain in his front paws, was tirelessly working on the chain with his teeth. The nanny goat that had nurtured Haqi to his maturity was kneeling by his side. No one knew when she had jumped over the fence of her pen and ended up on the deck. While Haqi was nibbling at the chain, the nanny kept licking his forehead and nasal bridge with the quivering tip of its tongue. When Haqi was tired and stopped to pant, the nanny would take over the job of biting the chain already burnished by Haqi's teeth…

"Gosh!" Mother's exclamation struck as being quivering.

Upon hearing Mother, the nanny goat turned its head, only to see the door of the bamboo house opened with the entire family emerging on the deck.

Widening its eyes, it gazed at them with trepidation.

Without warning, she rushed over and bleating and dropped to her front knees before Guoha and his parents.

Baa! Baa!

The goat mother was begging them to take the chain off its kid's neck!

She would rather die than see the kid that she had brought up struggling in pain.

Father threw himself over the moaning Haqi and huddled him in his arms as if he had gone crazy.

"Haqi! Oh, Haqi! It's not that I'm ruthless. It's the world that won't tolerate you…"

It was the first time for Guoha to hear his father sobbing.

Chapter 11

A few days later, Haqi's wound was completely healed.

Guoha's family had a long and difficult discussion and finally decided to release him in the Motagu Forest to roam freely in the place where his parents had lived.

Haqi was a grownup after all and should become a member of the jungle as a real leopard.

They decided to release him far away from home.

This would prevent not only the Manzhe Stockade snappers from locating Haqi but also Haqi from finding his way back.

Carrying his hunting rifle and provisions with him, Father led Haqi to the Motagu Forest and plodded in it for eight days and eight nights.

He observed Haqi's every move and, wherever it left a mark, he would stealthily pour a little turpentine over it to mask its scent.

Only in this way could Father stop Haqi from tracing his way back home.

But, no matter how hard he tried, Father could not shake Haqi off.

Haqi followed and watched him closely every step of the way.

Judging by how Haqi looked, Father could tell that he was not aware that the purpose of this trip was to let him go for good. He trailed Father so closely simply because he was worried about him. He feared that mishap might occur to Father in this endless primeval forest.

He was guarding Father with full devotion.

Father felt both awkward and sad.

Several times did he fumble for the leather rope tucked over his waist. He wanted to lasso Haqi and tie him to a tree without his notice before pulling himself away.

But each time, he failed to untie the leather rope.

He was worrying that a loose noose would not be able to restrain Haqi at all whereas a tight one would simply starve him to death in the old-growth forest in case he could not break loose.

When seeing a wild rabbit darting by, Father finally had an idea.

He pretended to run after the rabbit but intentionally kept a distance from it.

He then called Haqi for help, "Haqi! Hurry! Go and get it! On the double!"

Haqi was taken in and went all out to chase the rabbit.

Meanwhile, Father figured out the wind direction and, with agonizing determination, headed for the depth of the forest in the wind.

Father shook off Haqi at long last.

He struggled back alone to the stockade, feeling as exhausted as if he had had only half life left in him.

His clothes had been tattered by branches and scratched by thorns; and his face, hands, and legs were covered with numerous bloody cuts and marks of bug bites. His bloodshot eyes were as red as hawthorn berries. He was so feeble that a breeze would have swept him off his feet.

He could not say a word. After gulping down three gourd-ladles of cold water, he threw himself onto the floor bed and fell asleep. He slumbered for the next three days and nights.

"I…I've finally sent Haqi to where he should be…"

After he came back to, Father murmured, a slight hint of a smile breaking on his dramatically thinned face.

Deep that night, someone tapped on the bamboo door of Guoha's house.

Father pulled himself up, opened the door, and peeped out…

"Yikes!"

With his scream, Father collapsed at the doorway.

Standing at the door was no stranger. It was none other than Haqi, whom Father proclaimed to have shaken off.

Haqi gave a shudder when he saw Father opening the door. He quickly extended his neck and got hold of the bottom of Father's trousers in his mouth.

Boo-hoo! A groan escaped from Haqi's throat.

Father saw clearly that Haqi was shedding tears like a human being in the bright moonlight…

Father was about to call him when Haqi flopped to the ground with a thump.

Father was terrified.

"My fault! It was my fault!"

He hurriedly stooped to hold Haqi in his arms.

Haqi had fainted from hunger.

What had happened in the forest after Haqi found himself abandoned by Father?

After catching the wild rabbit, Haqi had returned, only

to find Father was nowhere to be found. He had been so frantic that he leapt up and down for a second.

He had been totally unprepared for what Father had done to him, thinking that they had simply crossed each other on their paths.

The forest had been so thick that he had feared that any mishap might have occurred to Father.

Growling and leaping, Haqi milled anxiously around in the forest.

He was bent on finding Father.

He wanted to protect him.

But he could not locate him.

Escaping in the wind, Father had left no odor behind him.

Frustrated over the failure to find Father, Haqi refused to eat and drink for a few days and nights.

He was so starved that his ribs were visible through the skin his sides.

He was so scrawny that his spine looked razor sharp.

With extraordinary stamina and alarming skills, he eventually returned to the stockade after making a long, strenuous journey.

While scratching the door, he had decided that he would rather die of hunger on the deck than eat anything if he learned that Father had not returned from the forest.

Father had surprised him when he opened the door.

For a moment, Haqi could not have believed his eyes.

So, Father is back? He asked himself.

And he is safe?

That was why he had grabbed the bottom of Father's trousers. He had wanted to verify what he had seen.

Sensing the familiar odor of Father, Haqi had been unable to keep the tears from swelling up in his eyes.

Not until then had he felt fatigued and hungry.

With a thump, he had collapsed.

Haqi was back.

He could leave neither Guoha's family nor his goat mother.

In fact, Guoha and his parents found it equally hard to tear themselves away from Haqi.

They had exhausted all possible alternatives when they had decided to release him to the wild.

During the days when Father had taken Haqi away, Guoha had cried as many times as he had lost count.

He had not been in a mood to eat the most favorite dishes that his mother had fixed for him.

Holding her tears back, Mother had tried to coax him to eat something. During the meantime, she spotted the nanny goat bleating toward the vacant deck without eating and drinking. Seeing this, Mother could no longer keep her tears from rolling down.

However, on the third day of Haqi's return, something went wrong again.

Chapter 12

That evening, Haqi was prowling for food in the forest when an arrow flew at him.

Aimed at his eye socket, this arrow was meant to be lethal.

Haqi ducked, and it missed his eyes but pierced one of his ears.

Ouch!

Haqi gave a screech, holding his head high.

He spied the archer behind a tree!

It was a man dressed in black cloth garments, his swarthy face matching the color of his attire!

Haqi was aware that this man was harming him.

Haqi stood fast gazing at him instead of charging over.

He was by no means afraid of the man, but, on the contrary, the man feared him.

While Haqi stayed put, the man panicked, so much so that, crowing like a chicken, he scurried into the forest, his hands covering the top of his head. The leaves rustled behind him as he bumped his way through the forest.

Haqi did not chase him, puzzled by many questions:

It was clearly a human being, wasn't it?

Why did he try to hurt me in the dark?

Wasn't he kind-hearted?

So, are people categorized into the kind and the unkind?

Haqi found it hard to get answers to the questions.

He had been raised by humans and living among them since infancy.

All humans had been equally kind-hearted in his eyes.

In the previous incident, when his leg had been injured, he had not expected a shot to have been fired by a human being. He had thought that he had stumbled on something mysterious.

Therefore, the sight of a human being shooting at him really stunned him.

He had not been able to figure out what had been on that man's mind.

He had interrupted his hunting and returned to the deck sullenly, with the arrow in his ear.

Seeing he had been wounded again, Guoha and his parents were very sad.

Father gingerly removed the arrow from his ear.

"This is not an arrow used by the Manzhe Stockade residents."

His hands trembling, Father realized that those from the Manzhe Stockade were not the only people who wanted to take Haqi's life.

It was lucky that the arrow had not been laced with the "poison of instant death."

Otherwise, Haqi would not have been able to come home.

Father's heart was trembling.

Haqi! Oh, Haqi! Living among humans, you seem to be living in the forest of knives. Many more people are after your life.

Haqi! Oh, Haqi! You may be harmless to anyone, but people of ill intentions will never spare you simply because you are a leopard with a fine coat and useful bones.

If we chain you home, you'll protest; if we send you back to the forest, you'll return; and if we set you free, you'll be killed by someone…

Well, there may be a thousand paths leading to a high mountain and ten thousand to an old forest, but I can't take a single step forward now.

Father was agonizing when thumping and thumping there came Uncle Tezhang up the wooden ladder.

He was holding a newspaper in his hand. "Hey, 'when a magpie's going to lay eggs, the nest is already available for her on a tree.' This time, we'll have the best home available for Haqi!" His loud voice preceded him into the bamboo house.

His resounding exclamation came as long-awaited rain in a drought season. The whole family gathered around him.

Beaming with joy, Uncle Tezhang unfolded the newspaper before them.

The newspaper was full of printed texts of Chinese characters.

Among them, there was a picture of an adorable panda cub.

Pointing at the cub with his thick fingers, Uncle Tezhang said, "Don't you see? The newspaper says that an old farmer with the family name Wang caught this 'little patterned bear' and sent it to a safari park. He's not only made headline news on a national newspaper but also been rewarded with some cash."

Guoha and his parents exclaimed in unison, "A safari park?"

"Yes, a safari park. If I hadn't picked up the newspaper, I wouldn't have remembered there's such a great place. My memory almost failed me."

A man of the world, Uncle Tezhang told Guoha and his parents what he had seen with some smugness, "The year I went to the capital of the province, I visited the safari park. It had a lot of animals, none of which were chained or tethered. They were enjoying themselves freely on the hill. They were fed with fish and other delicious meaty food. They were even offered eggs to eat. The zookeepers gave them regular physical exams. If an animal fell ill, they would treat it with drugs or injections or sent for a doctor. Well, their care was so thorough that no one had a chance to harm the animals. Neither could anyone lay a finger on them."

Guoha burst out with joy, "Wow, there's such a great place for animals!"

"Sure, it's really a great place!" Mother added.

Guoha's eyes flickered to reveal their brilliance. "Uncle Tezhang, you mean we can also send Haqi to the safari park?"

"Sure, sure!" Grinning from ear to ear, Uncle Tezhang nodded and said, "It is high time Haqi enjoyed his life there. He's gotten a long one before him. If you miss him, save your money and pay him a visit. Then, I'll be your guide. Well, it's funny to recall my visit to the safari park. I saw a big rhino facing the other way from the visitors watching it and sticking its tail up. I knew it was going to pee. So I yelled to the spectators to try to scatter them. But, none of the colorfully dressed city dwellers caught what I said. They were still foolhardily clustering together talking and laughing with wide-opened mouths when the big rhino began to release itself. Gosh! The pee was gushing out like running water from a tap, and its torrent sent the crowd scurrying in all directions. I saw with my own eyes that some of them got the pee into their mouth and swallowed it. Those city dwellers, if they had never seen a rhino, they should have seen a cow or an ox, right? They are all bovines to me anyway. When an animal of this kind sticks up its tail, it's going to either pooh or pee. How could they be so ignorant that they would not dodge? Hahaha, the safari park is full of fun. So, I strongly suggest that you send Haqi there."

Mother beamed, her eyes narrowed to slits, saying, "It's like 'a pillow's readily there when you feel sleepy.' This comes really handy. Let's send Haqi there. It's better than anywhere else."

Guoha asked, "But how are we going to send him since we've never been to the park?"

Uncle Tezhang smirked and said, "Well, we don't have to send him. According to the paper, the farmer Wang had written a letter to the park to tell them what he was up to. The park then dispatched a truck to pick up the 'little patterned bear.' One year, while I was forging knives in Nanla, I saw the safari park trucking wild bulls. They had a huge wooden cage on the truck and coaxed the bull into it before they let down the iron door. Then the truck got off with wisps of smoke trailing from its butt. It's really a cinch."

A lively conversation went on while Father squatting aside in silence with his eyes fixed on the newspaper.

Mother nudged him with her hand and asked, "Hey, there! We've been rattling here like mad, but why are you so mum?"

Father remained tacit.

With widened eyes, he gazed at the panda picture.

Acting like a spoiled child, Guoha shook his father saying, "Dad, please say something. Do you agree to send Haqi to the park or not?"

"Big bro," said Uncle Tezhang as he inched closer to Father, "I take it as a good thing. Otherwise, why should there be the newspaper report and the reward?"

Breathing a heavy sigh, Father began unhurriedly, "As goats clamber up a steep slope only to get to eat new grass, so we are after neither newspapers exposure nor rewards. We want nothing but a good and safe place for Haqi. I think we can do it since he'll be free from hunger, cold, and human bullies, and since we can visit him when we miss him."

Uncle Tezhang extended Father's sentiment further by saying, "If you think we can do it, let's do it fast. How about you writing to the safari park this evening. As it happens, my cousin is going back home tomorrow, and we can ask her to take the letter to the prefectural capital and mail it out in a post office there."

"Mhm," Father nodded and said, "Fine, I'll write the letter. Mail it and wait to see how the safari park will respond."

That evening, Father asked an elderly man in the stockade with the best penmanship to write the letter for him, with Uncle Tezhang as a consultant for needed information. Clustering around the fire pit, Guoha and his parents all contributed to the wording of the letter, which would decide the fate of Haqi.

The next day, the entire family came to Uncle Tezhang. Father handed the critical letter to Tezhang's cousin Asha with both hands.

Witnessing Asha tucking the letter in her satchel, Guoha was still a bit worried. He cautioned her, "Aunt, please don't lose it!"

Asha burst into a smile, "Mhm, you may rest assured."

Chapter 13

About ten days after Asha's departure, a truck with a canvas canopy came sputtering to the entrance of the stockade.

The truck carried a huge wooden cage on it and had big white letters prominently printed on each of its doors, which read "Safari Park."

The unexpected turn of events both surprised and delighted Guoha and his parents.

The entire stockade was alive with excitement. The villagers, old and young, turned out and clogged around the truck.

Two middle-aged men dressed in blue uniforms got off the truck. The tall man was named Zhang, and the short one, Liu.

Tall Man Zhang grinned as he shook Father's hand, saying, "We thank you on behalf of all the staff of our safari park!"

With this, he produced a letter of introduction from his pocket and handed it to Father.

Guoha moved closer to his father and caught sight of a sharp, big, red official seal of "Safari Park" towards the bottom of the letter.

"Brother, we'll take Haqi with us first. In a couple of days, we'll send for you and drive you to our safari park for a visit and see if Haqi lives happily or not. We'll hold a public meeting to commend you for wildlife protection. At the meeting, we'll give you an award and a prize. Brother, get your ethnic costumes ready for the occasion."

Upon hearing the remark, the crowd burst into cheers.

Tezhang's wife elbowed to the front and yelled, "It was my husband Tezhang who came up with the idea to send Haqi to the safari park. The letter you received had been brought to the prefecture capital by my husband Tezhang's cousin. To invite people to the park for fun, you mustn't leave us two behind…"

Before she finished, Uncle Tezhang squeezed his way to her side and gave her a tug, so forceful that it sat her on the ground.

The move, however, did not stop her from ranting, "And

we must share the cash award…"

"Folks! Folks!" shouted the short man, holding both his hands up in the air. "We'll sent for a big bus to pick up not only Guoha's family but also the representatives of your stockade. We're giving awards to both Guoha's family and the entire stockade!"

The on-looking crowd became more joyous.

Guoha and his mother hugged each other with excitement.

Only Father did not have a smile on his face. He said in a low, resonant voice, "We're after nothing but a good place for Haqi to live a peaceful life. We're happy as long as he's treated well after you take him with you."

"Don't worry, bro," said Tall Man Zhang as he patted Father on his shoulder. "When you come to visit us and see the safari park with your own eyes, you'll be less worried. The living conditions for the wildlife there are among the best of the safari parks in the country."

Short Man Liu then asked, "Hey, where's Haqi now? How about taking us to him?"

Shaking his head, Father replied, "You'd better wait. He's sleeping on the deck now and would be startled by strangers. Besides, this wooden cage, you'd better let our people handle it. Otherwise, Haqi would get suspicious and refuse to get in."

"Yes, yes," Short Man Liu nodded, "We already anticipated that. We can't force Haqi into the cage. We must go slow so he won't be skeptical. We aren't going into your house then."

"Please," Uncle Tezhang cut in. "You two are welcome to my house. You may put up for the night there. I've been to your safari park…"

With this, he took them away with him.

Several stout young men unloaded the cage from the truck.

The wooden cage was solidly made with an iron cage door that had a latch on it.

The sight of the cage suddenly deprived Guoha of all his joy somehow.

Haqi will be put in this cage, he thought, and carried to the faraway provincial capital, where he'll be separated from us forever.

Does he like it?

But, what else can we do if he doesn't?

"Aw, poor Haqi…," sighed Guoha.

Father surveyed the wooden cage from top to bottom and felt it hard to get Haqi into it.

After pondering for a while, he said to the young men, "To coax him into it, I think we must decorate it to make it look like our bamboo house."

Working together, they soon camouflaged the cage…

It had a thatched gable roof, walls of bamboo fences, and a door that looked like as if it were opened in a bamboo house when lifted.

With a pull of the switch from outside, the iron door would

fall and shut Haqi inside.

The noise created by transporting this "mini bamboo house" to the deck woke Haqi up with a start.

Widening his eyes, he gazed at the new house with amazement.

Father said to Guoha, "With so many people here, Haqi will never get into the cage. We'll go to Uncle Tezhang's house to join the guests. Try to get him in yourself because you're best friends, and your command will work the best. Tell him this is the new house we've built for him, and it'll shelter him from stormy rains. Let the door fall as soon as he gets in."

Father led the rest of the people away with him.

Only Guoha remained with Haqi on the deck.

Haqi was still fixing his eyes on the "mini bamboo house," which seemed to appeal to him as he walked around it snuffing every now and then.

Haqi stroked his forehead and said tenderly, "Hi Haqi, Father built this bamboo house for you so that you don't have to sleep on the deck even in a storm. This bamboo house will be your new home. So, please…please hurry and get in…"

Guoha could not go on.

He felt deeply grieved.

It was the first time for him to trick Haqi.

Haqi looked up and stared at him.

Guoha quickly looked away.

He saw Haqi's eyes filled with trust and dependence.

Without the guts to look into them, he hurriedly lowered his head.

However, Guoha felt that he could not go on like this. If Haqi was not put in the cage, how could he be carried away?

Poor Haqi!

Hardening his heart, Guoha placed his hands on the buttocks of Haqi and, as he pushed, said "Haqi, get in quickly and see if it's big enough for you to sleep in."

Haqi took a step forward and balked.

He looked back at Guoha in silence.

Guoha felt that his look had read his mind.

Forcing a smile, he said, "Haqi, so you don't trust me? Here, I'll show you how to get in myself."

With this, Guoha crawled into the "mini bamboo house."

Haqi followed him but stopped short outside the door, peering into the cage with curiosity.

"Come, Haqi! In here! Come in!" said Guoha waving his young hand.

Finally, Haqi dragged himself into the cage.

He felt it hard to reject Guoha's repeated calls, but by getting himself into the cage, he would forfeit his freedom for the rest of his life.

Haqi and Guoha lay side by side.

Taking a look at Haqi, Guoha sat up. To calm Haqi down, he started grooming him, as he had usually done on the deck.

Haqi felt so much at ease that he squinted his eyes.

But, his pointed ears were still pricked up vigilantly

trying to catch any unusual sound.

He would instantly leap out of the confinement once there was a stir.

Guoha knew that Haqi had never been off guard. He kept scratching him casually.

While combing Haqi's coat with his hands, Guoha began to babble on silently.

Haqi, oh Haqi! Do you know this is the last time I'm scratching you? You'll be trucked away to the faraway provincial capital tomorrow morning. Who knows if we can see each other again or not? Even if we can, I'm not certain if the staff in the safari park will allow me to touch you. You'll likely forget me after three or five years of good life in the park. Then, when I try to groom you, you'll probably bite me. Haqi, don't forget me, please. You don't, right? I won't forget you, either. When you're gone, I'll miss you…"

Just then, people were heard coming from a distance.

Haqi pricked up his ears further.

Guoha knew that he could not keep grooming him like this anymore.

He said to Haqi in silence, "Haqi, I'm terribly sorry for deceiving you. Please pardon me, please, please…"

Repeating his apologies silently, Guoha withdrew himself from the cage with great caution.

He had just gotten out of the cage when Haqi turned around and fixed his starry eyes upon him.

Guoha's hand on the latch trembled.

But, Haqi did not rush out of the "mini bamboo house." He lay there motionless, staring fixedly at Guoha.

His innocent, sparkling eyes were still overflowing with trust.

Guoha's hand quivered more vehemently.

His heart was pounding...

Why must we put Haqi in the cage?

Why do we have to send him away?

Ah, humans, I beg you to show your compassion!

Please don't even think of harming Haqi again. Please keep him with us here!

You know this is his home...

Haqi, get out quickly! I'm going to shut the door.

When I do, you can never come out again...

...No! No! You can't get out! You can't! If you do, you'll get killed by some humans.

We shut you in because we want to keep you alive.

Do you know that?

Do you understand?

Can you pardon me...?

Bump!

The door fell shut as Guoha let his hand go involuntarily.

It was let down like a collapsing mountain.

For a moment, Guoha could see nothing but darkness.

Grrrrrrrr!

He heard Haqi's calling.

He felt a draft of warm breath blasting his way.

He opened his eyes, only to see Haqi standing in front of him, his face against his.

Only that there was the iron fence door separating them…

A cold iron door!

Grrrrrrr…

Haqi growled.

He could not comprehend why the door should have dropped and was keeping him apart from Guoha.

He stared at Guoha in silence behind the iron door.

He thought that Guoha was playing hide-and-seek with him, as they had done previously in the woods.

He enjoyed frolicking with Guoha because they had been playing together since he was a cub. They had become the best playmates.

But, no! No! This time, Haqi realized: it's no child's play.

This is real! This is real!

Guoha turned abruptly and dashed down the stairs of the bamboo house, his hands over his face.

He scudded forward. He kept running.

He had no intention to stop.

He did not want to stop at all.

He wished he would bump straight into a tree and kill himself.

That was because he heard clearly the heartbreaking commotion behind him…

Noises of people around the abominable wooden cage were drifting into his ears.

They tore down the camouflage to reveal the wooden cage's vicious true feature.

They put an iron lock on the door to deprive Haqi of his freedom.

Having suddenly realized his situation, Haqi started calling Guoha at the top of his lungs, wretchedly begging him.

Guoha pressed his hands over his ears, and he pressed hard, wishing that he would never hear anything.

Guoha shut his eyes, and he shut them tight, wishing that they would never see anything…

Evening came. Guoha did not go home.

He took refuge from the horrible site in an elderly man's house at the end of the stockade.

But, he was wide awake the whole night.

He covered his eyes, but Haqi's face was always flashing before them.

He covered his ears, but Haqi's howling was constantly resonating by them.

He learned later that his parents had not passed the night at home, either.

It was because the wooden cage imprisoning Haqi was right on the deck.

Only the nanny goat that had brought Haqi up was keeping

him accompany throughout the night of misery and solitude.

Upon hearing the abnormal wailing from Haqi, the nanny goat had jumped out of its pen and leapt up to the deck.

It was taken aback at the sight of Haqi locked up in the wooden cage.

It knew that it was unable to open the cage to free its kid on its own.

It came near the cage and dropped to its knees bleating.

It hoped that Guoha and his parents could come out to help it rescue Haqi.

However, despite its prolonged bleating, nothing happened in the house.

It pulled itself up and pushed the bamboo door open with its horns, only to find the room dark and vacant.

Poor nanny! Who in the world could share your motherly pain?

For the whole night, Haqi kept up his lugubrious and heart-wrenching howls.

Again and again, the nanny licked Haqi's forehead and nasal bridge behind the fence door.

Over and over, it gnawed at the abominable wooden rails of the cage along with Haqi.

They left their tooth marks on every rail…

And each mark was stained with blood.

The next morning, when the truck roared queerly, it took Uncle Tezhang to exert extraordinary effort to pull the nanny goat away from Haqi.

Baa-Baa-Baa…

Grrrr-grrrr-grrrr…

The wooden cage was loaded to the truck.

The forcefully separated mother and son were crying mournfully.

The truck was sputtering jarringly.

And it spewed black smoke from its butt.

The nanny goat looked as if it had known that it was the last chance to be with its kid.

It was seeking the only people that could come to her kid's rescue among the crowd that turned out to see Haqi off.

But it was disappointed.

It could not find the most familiar faces.

It could not hear the most familiar voices.

Where are they hiding! She was wondering.

Don't they know that Haqi is locked up in the wooden cage and being taken away soon?

Why don't they come out to Haqi's rescue?

Are they less courageous than a nanny like me?

It looked around with its entreating eyes as if to say:

Who can stand up and set my kid free?

If a life must be imprisoned in a cage, then lock me up.

I beg all of you! Please let Haqi out!

Vroom! Vroom!

Finally, the truck began to roll.

Tears began to stream from the nanny goat's eyes...

With the bumping of the truck, Haqi was quivering all over.

His paws on the rails, Haqi stretched his neck and peered down into the crowd.

In fact, he had been searching around with his eyes numerous times.

But, he did not want to give up.

He wished that the entire family of Guoha would have popped up from a crack in the ground so that he could take a final look at them. He would not care if they looked fussy as long as they were them.

But in the end, he was as disappointed as his goat mother.

He gradually clenched his jaws and clenched them tighter and tighter.

It was beyond his comprehension:

Why did they refuse to show up?

Why did they shun me?

Why did they dupe me?

Have they had a change of heart?

So kind-hearted people can change their hearts?

If humans can change their hearts, I hate them! I hate humans!

The truck rumbled away, carrying with it a thumping heart of hatred.

The criminal end part of the canvas canopy fell and shielded Haqi's eyesight.

Haqi could see nothing.

There was nothing but the darkness imbued with the pungent odor of gasoline around Haqi.

He felt suffocated.

He roared angrily.

His anger stemmed more from his revolutionary recognition of human beings than his desire for freedom...

You've turned your back on me, but why did you bring me up in the first place?

So, you don't think we animals have feelings just because we cannot walk on two legs and talk as you do?

Then, you can torment me in such a cruel way?

Haqi began to detest Guoha's family. He had lavished his affection upon them, but they...

Haqi! Ah, Haqi! You are wrong in your judgment!

He did not know that far, far away from the stockade and by the narrow mountain path, the only way that the truck was supposed to pass, stood the Guoha family. They stood silently under the ring-cupped oak trees swaying in the wind. They were peering intensely toward the stockade.

It was the zenith of the hills surrounding their stockade.

From here, they could see the truck not only leaving the stockade but also circling around on the mountain road leading to the other side.

They had arrived before daybreak.

They had been standing silently under the oak trees, regardless of the mountain dews wetting their clothes and the mountain wind disheveling their hair.

They stood motionless, gazing and gazing into the direction of the stockade with wide-open eyes overwhelmed with tears.

They had seen the truck moving.

They had seen it rolling out of the stockade.

They had seen it climbing up onto the mountain road.

Now they saw it coming by!

With deafening rumbling, it rolled over the hearts of Guoha, Father, and Mother toward the misty and cloudy mountains in the distance.

Haqi! Ah, Haqi…

Chapter 14

After a bumpy day, the truck stopped toward the evening at a cluster-fig tree that looked like a huge umbrella.

A stilted wooden building stood alone on the waist of a slope by the tree.

The house was walled with pine planks and roofed with thatch. It was a humble economical inn.

A boy looking either twelve or thirteen came out to greet the guests.

He was lanky, his big eyes ping-ponging like meteors. He wore a collarless, long-sleeve shirt that opened in the front on his upper body and a patterned puttees of blue cloth around his legs.

His costume told that he was from the Yao ethnic group.

"Where're your parents?" asked the driver Tall Man Zhang sticking his head out of the opening as he had pushed the truck's door ajar.

The boy answered as his eyes blinked, "My mom's gone to visit our relatives. Father left this afternoon for the plain to buy salt, and he'll be back early tomorrow morning. With me at home, even hawks flying over from afar can still find their nest to perch. Get off your truck, and I'll sure fix you a good meal and get you a room for a sound sleep. I'll guarantee that you can set out in high spirits tomorrow morning."

"Wow, I didn't expect an early teen to have been so glib-tongued," said Short Man Liu, who then patted Tall Man Zhang on his back. "Let's put up for the night here. Larger hotels are still over a steep slope. Since it's getting dark, we'd better not take any risk."

Tall Man Zhang nodded, shut the engine, and jumped off the truck.

"Hey, little Yao boy! What's your name?"

"My name is Duolong."

"Duolong? Mhm, it sounds great, meaning 'More Prosperous'."

"Thank you, uncle!"

"Wow, you're a polite boy. Duolong, do you have liquor at home?"

"Yes! My dad's brewed a lot of corn wine. It's great! We also have barbecued muntjac meat in big chunks. They're all cooked perfectly!"

Short Man Liu who was trailing Tall Man Zhang said grinning, "That's great! That's awesome! Get us both the wine and the meat. We'll pay you handsomely."

"Besides, Duolong," said Tall Man Zhang pointing at the truck. "Get a large piece of raw muntjac meat and feed Haqi on the truck. Put it on the same check."

"Aah?" Duolong gasped in astonishment, "What? Haqi? And he eats raw meat?"

"Hahaha!" Short Man Liu burst into a laugher, saying, "It's a leopard. It's called Haqi, the same way you're called Duolong. Don't be afraid! Just go and feed it. It's locked up in a wooden cage. Besides, even if it's set free, it won't bite you because it has been raised by humans. It's a donation from an Aini family, a lovely family. Hahaha!"

Being a talker, Short Man Liu could hardly stop once he started a conversation.

He would have babbled on but for a leer cast by Tall Man Zhang.

Nothing can keep a boy from being curious.

Duolong hurriedly poured water for the two guests to wash their faces, served them the wine and barbecue, and took a large piece of raw meat to the truck.

He lifted the canopy up and saw the dejected Haqi curling up into a bundle.

Grrrrr…

Haqi caught sight of Duolong, too.

He growled. Ah, a boy! A boy like Guoha!

Handing the meat into the wooden cage, Duolong said in a hushed voice, "Haqi, you must be starved. Here's something for you to eat!"

Haqi snuffed at the meat.

"Haqi, why don't you eat?" Duolong asked warmly.

Kids are innate communicators with animals.

Duolong believed that Haqi could understand him.

"Hurry and eat, Haqi!" Holding the wooden rails of the cage, Duolong cajoled with patience, "Coming a long way, aren't you feeling hungry? Do…do you suspect that the meat is poisoned? Don't be afraid. How can I poison the meat? Look here! I'll give it a lick first!"

With this, Duolong began licking the meat.

Haqi's widened his eyes followed Duolong's every move.

"See? It's good. Please eat now." As he said, Duolong held the meat to Haqi.

Haqi still would not eat.

He was not in the mood.

Duolong realized that the leopard was distressed.

He remembered catching and caging a little red bird once. Like Haqi, the bird had refused to eat or drink. His father had told him that the little red bird had been in distress. If it had not been set free, it would have been starved or stressed to death. Inspired by his father's words, he had released the little red bird. He had watched the bird flying away joyously and then alighting on a tree branch. He had seen it soon picking up a worm from a leaf and swallowing it.

His recollection prompted him to focus his eyes on the cage's iron lock.

Yes! This leopard must be as stressed up as the little red bird.

How miserable he is, curling up into a small bundle as if he were sick!

Just then, Duolong heard something like wrangling between the two men in the wooden building. Then, a thump that sounded like a tree falling on the floor.

What was going on?

He rushed up to the wooden building, pushed the door open, and caught sight of the tall man sprawling on the floor. He had passed out from alcohol, his head and face splashed with wine.

The short man was still gulping the wine from a big bowl held in both hands.

Seeing Duolong enter the room, he put the bowl down, looked straight into his eyes, and began to address him, his head shaking and his lips quivering involuntarily. He said, "Come over! Come here! Drink with me. Look at him! Isn't he worthless? He may be as tall as a pole, but he's good for nothing! He's passed out and is lying spread-eagle like this after only two bowls of this cat's pee. And he should have had the guts to challenge me to drink more. What does he know? Perhaps he can't even tell if a horse has a long face and an ox has curved horns. Without the information I had told him, what could he have accomplished? Nothing! Even though he has the truck and drives it! Even if he could conjure up big red flowers from thin air, who would have been so foolish as to put stashes of cash in his hands?" Then, turning to the man on the ground, he went on raving, "How can you turn your back on a partner as soon as you've made a fortune? Where's your conscience? Where's your sense of right and wrong...?"

After finishing what sounded like nonsense, the short man resumed drinking, covering his face with the bowl.

The wine leaked from the corners of his mouth and ran down his neck. Not bothering to wipe it off, he refilled the bowl without delay.

The short man's state of drunkenness amused Duolong.

He may have seen many drunkards in this home-business inn before, but this was his first time seeing someone so inebriated.

He went up to him and said by mimicking his father's tone, "Hey, fella! You'd better drink a little less. Otherwise, you can't start off tomorrow."

"Drink less?" grumbled the short man as his drunken eyes struggled to focus on Duolong. He then went on in staccato, "It's you or me? Who must drink less? I'm feeling... happy...eh...content. I'd feel better...if I should be completely drunk."

"Judging from what you said, I can tell you must've made a fortune, eh? Congratulations then!"

"Oh, well, thanks! I'd be more than happy to share my feeling of joy with you," said the short man folding his hands to punctuate his sentiment. "A fortune! A real fortune! It's this much! This much!" Stretching out five fingers and flipping them once in front of Duolong, the short man told him, "A big five plus a small one: Altogether it's fifty-five hundred!"

Fifty-five hundred yuan? Duolong was alarmed and wondered: What kind of business has brought them such a fortune? Perhaps, they're doing something illegal like smuggling, aren't they?

"Yep..., you're right! Fifty-five thousand yuan! So, bring me as much wine and meat as you can. I've can pay you as much as you charge me. You know, it's that leopard... It... it's worth fifty-five thousand yuan! The buyer can get much more by selling it again. Hurry...go and get me the wine!"

What? The leopard? Haqi? Duolong could hardly believe his ears.

He couldn't help asking, "Uncle, isn't it the leopard donated to the safari park by an Aini family?"

"Haha! Haha!" The short man burst into a guffaw and said, "Donated to the safari park? I am the safari park! The park is me! Haha! Those people are as brainless as potatoes.

Tell them meat pies can fall from the sky and they would sew a sack to receive them. Haha! We're from the safari park? We're from nowhere. We're simply collectors of leopard skins! Hey, as it happened, I bumped into a silly woman on my way one day. She accosted me and asked me where the post office was. She told me she had an important letter to mail out. I was being smart and asked what was so important. She said that someone was going to give a leopard to a zoo. That someone had raised it since it was a cub. On hearing that, I was so happy that I almost bit my tongue off and swallowed it. I told her without delay that I was from the post office and on my way to work. With a few fibs here and there, I managed to cheat the silly woman of the letter. I opened it, and found what she had said was true and the opportunity to make big bucks. I hurried back to the provincial capital and told this 'pole man' everything." Then pointing with his protruding lips at the drunken tall man sprawling on the ground, he went on, "Ah, it was him. I told him about the leopard. I didn't expect him to be a worse conman than I am. He carved a fake official seal of the safari park out of a soap bar and wrote the name of the park on the truck doors with a worn-out brush dipped in white paint. He changed the license plate and drove the truck out of town. Hey! The tricks could only fool those country folks. Haha! We didn't expect that we could have so easily gotten the leopard onto our truck. You've already seen it with your own eyes, haven't you? I'm not bragging to you simply because you're young."

As he was babbling, he started singing at the top of his voice, "Ah-yi-ya, as peach flowers bloom, and apricot blossoms wither. Who calls the peach flowers Big Sisters? I do/Hey, Big Sisters, the lamb's being overcooked in the pot, Big Sisters…"

Duolong was so indignant that he felt as if his eyes had been spitting fire.

"Only a fool who lets go money when money is there. No one but a wise immortal like Zhuge Liang could manipulate Nature…" As he hummed and yelled alternately, the short man kept pouring wine from one big bowl to the other back and forth.

A moment after his drunken fit, he thumped to the ground.

Duolong spat into the faces of the two drunkards. He then went out of the wooden building, kerosene lantern in hand.

Duolong came to the truck and raised the lantern so that it shone upon the characters painted on the truck doors.

He remembered his father telling him that kerosene could remove paints. "Okay, I'll give it a try," he said to himself.

He poured a little kerosene from the lantern on the corner of his shirt's front part and rubbed it against the door. Sure enough, the characters were wiped off.

He also remembered his father saying that when wine was in, the truth was out. Duolong now believed that these two hooligans were doing something against reason and nature!

How can some people be so vicious in this world?

Then, what shall I do?

Grrrrr…

Haqi growled in a hushed voice on the truck.

He had heard the movement of a person off the truck and had been able to discern from the footfalls that it was the boy that had brought him meat.

The growl reminded Duolong of Haqi's danger. Yes! No matter what, I'll set the leopard free, as I did to the little red bird, Duolong said to himself. Since he's been raised by an Aini family, he sure knows how to get back to them.

On second thought, Duolong was seized with the fear that the two hooligans would not spare him when they sobered up and found out that he had let the leopard go.

Then, he was thinking, "How miserable it would be if poor Haqi were to be sold and resold like this!"

There was no time for worries. He decided to release Haqi and let fate take care of the rest.

After he made up his mind, he returned to the wooden building carrying the kerosene lantern.

Inside the house, the two drunkards were still sleeping like a log, and their snore was so loud that it could shake the mountains.

He found a key from the tall man's pocket.

Holding it tight in his hands, Duolong dashed out.

"Haqi! Haqi!" He whispered, "I'm here to get you out."

With a click, the iron door was unlocked.

Duolong pulled the door open and said, "Haqi, you're free. Go back home!"

Pleasantly surprised, Haqi leapt whooshing out of the wooden cage.

He trotted a couple of steps and sprang up in the air once before being convinced that he was indeed free.

He looked back, gurgling.

He did not know how to express his gratitude to this boy who had set him free.

Waving at Haqi, Duolong said encouragingly, "Haqi, hurry and go!"

But, Haqi did not budge.

He stood motionless for a while. Then he suddenly rushed to the tractor of the truck, where he stood up placing his front paws on the window and peeped into it.

"Ahh! You're looking for those two guys?" asked Duolong. Pointing at the wooden building, he continued, "They're lying drunk on the floor. So, go and hurry up!"

Haqi seemed to have understood Duolong and darted toward the wooden building.

Duolong followed him into it.

Haqi shuddered a little at seeing the two men on the floor and immediately started sniffing at the nostrils of them one by one.

Grrrr...

Haqi looked back at Duolong, his eyebrows twitching.

"You're worrying about me?" Duolong suddenly realized what Haqi was up to. "Haqi, you fear that the two hooligans would retaliate against me when they wake up, and that's why you're not running away. You want to stay here to protect me, right?"

Haqi listened attentively. After a while, he turned and headed out of the wooden building.

Duolong was about to step out in the wake of Haqi when suddenly he felt two big hands around his neck…

"Well, see what you've done to us! I'll choke you to death!"

It was the tall man who had cupped Duolong's neck with his hands.

No one knew when he had pulled himself up, his eyes bulging like those of a mad cow.

"Haqi…"

Duolong uttered a cry before seeing stars.

Haqi heard him and turned around.

The tall man was so frightened at the sight of Haqi that he involuntarily let go of Duolong and was about to turn and run.

How could Haqi let him flee? He pounced upon him and held his neck in his mouth until he gave up floundering.

Duolong found a rope and bound the man's hands and feet securely before Haqi loosened his mouth.

Haqi then picked up something from the floor with his mouth and then dropped it clicking before Duolong.

At a close look, Duolong saw, to his surprise, the iron lock that had been used to fasten the wooden cage.

"Haqi, you're awesome! You mean we drag these two hooligans into the cage and lock them up, right? Okay! Let's do it!"

With Haqi's help, Duolong hauled the two ruffians into the wooden cage.

Even by now, the short man was still fast asleep.

Click!

Duolong locked the wooden cage.

Still concerned over Duolong's safety, Haqi walked around the cage twice before parting.

Duolong said, "Haqi, hurry back to your family! When my dad's back, we'll take the two men to your stockade to let them admit their guilt. Men of wicked heart will come to no good end."

Chapter 15

Haqi set out.

He galloped along the moonlit mountain path where he had come from by trailing the odor given off by the tires of the truck.

He was gulping the fresh air of freedom that filled the mountains and plains.

He had never felt that he was so agile.

At the speed he was running, he would be able to reach the stockade before daybreak. He would suddenly appear before Guoha's family to give them a happy surprise.

No, that was impossible. He would by instinct roar the moment he saw the stockade at a distance, way before he climbed up to Guoha's bamboo house. His rumbling roar would wake the entire stockade up from their slumber…

However, the villagers were still sleeping like babies at daybreak.

Their sweet dreams were disturbed by no sound.

Squeak!

The door of Guoha's house was pushed open.

Father stepped out rubbing his eyes that had stayed open all of the night.

The banana grove stood silently in the dense fog.

Father sighed as he gazed melancholy at nothing toward the banana grove.

In his mind's eye, he saw Haqi's father delivering him to the bamboo house via the grove.

Time elapsed so fast that Haqi had grown into a big leopard.

After all, we haven't let his parents down, he thought.

Well, how faraway is Haqi being taken now?

He must have gotten over the Nanla Mountain.

Father was seized with sadness at the thought of Haqi.

He did not have the heart to turn to look at the deck where Haqi had rested.

But, he could not help casting his eyes at it as he had been so used to doing.

He suddenly blurted out, "Haqi!"

On hearing the cry, Guoha and his mother rushed squeezing out of the bamboo door together.

"Where? Where's Haqi?" the amazed son and mother asked in unison.

There was not a soul of Haqi on the deck.

But the entire family were dazed as they stared with their widened eyes at the deck.

On the straw-littered deck lay a gorgeous golden tail of a leopard!

It was Haqi's!

Around it were distinct muddy paw prints.

The prints were back and forth and overlaid many times.

They had been left by Haqi!

It was evident that Haqi had been here.

He had come back home.

He had been back to the deck.

He had paced back and forth silently close to his loved ones who had raised him as a family member.

Two paw prints were left conspicuously in front of the bamboo door.

But, in the end, he had decided not to scratch it.

He had been contemplating painfully.

He had been agonizing over choices.

Finally, he had bitten his tail off and left it on the deck as an eternal memorabilia to his loved ones. He had then departed ruefully…

He had lost his trust in his loved ones.

He had misunderstood his loved ones who were kind-hearted.

How traumatic his pacing had been!

What a harrowing memorabilia!

"Haqi…"

Guoha and his parents called in chorus.

They looked fixedly at the tail on the deck.

Haqi, you are gone, and in such a quiet manner.

How much you would have wanted to tell us, and how much we would have liked to say to you!

But, you didn't say anything.

And you left feeling wronged and hurt. And you left in silence.

Don't you know that in this human world, evildoers may sometimes not get punished while those who do good deeds may often be misunderstood?

But, in the end, evil will be condemned and good will be commended.

Haqi, you shouldn't have gone like this.

The emotional trauma that your departure has caused your loved ones will be indelible.

Where did you go?

Where...where are you now?

Baa-baa...

Faint and yet doleful bleats drifted from outside the stockade.

It came from Haqi's goat mother.

Breaking off their ruminations as if waking up from a dream, they dashed down the stairs of the bamboo house and, following the bleats, to the outskirt of the stockade.

There, they saw the nanny standing alone on a precipitous cliff, as petrified as a white statue of holy purity. She was gazing toward the gloomy Motagu Forest.

Mountain wind swept over from the forest, swaying tens of thousands of trees and rustling many more of their leaves.

Suddenly, the agonizing family of Guoha came to the realization that the Motagu Forest was beckoning them.

And, they could hear clearly the profoundly affectionate call of the Motagu Forest:

Come over...come over...come over...

Written in the western suburbs of Beijing on April 10, 1982.

Rewritten on April 13, 2018.